Honey Bunch AND Norman

The HONEY BUNCH AND NORMAN *Series*

By Helen Louise Thorndyke

Honey Bunch
AND Norman

By
HELEN LOUISE THORNDYKE

NEW YORK
Grosset & Dunlap
PUBLISHERS

Honey Bunch and Norman

CONTENTS

Contents

Honey Bunch AND Norman

CHAPTER I

ANIMAL ACTORS

"OH, PLEASE stand up on your hind legs," Honey Bunch Morton begged her police dog puppy, "or we can't be in the May Day parade."

The little blond-haired, blue-eyed girl had been trying for ten minutes to teach the puppy this trick. But he was not doing very well.

Norman Clark, her playmate, was looking on. "Maybe your puppy wants a reward," he suggested. "I'll get him a bone."

The two children were in Honey Bunch's back yard. Right now it was filled with neighborhood boys and girls. They were busily pounding and cutting large sheets of cardboard with hammers and saws. Here and there open paint boxes lay on the ground.

Honey Bunch and Norman were in charge of a float the children were making for the parade. The scene on the float was to be *Hi diddle diddle*. Honey Bunch's puppy would be the dog that "laughed to see such sport."

"Laugh!" Norman urged the dog. "If you do, I'll give you a bone."

Norman was chubby and freckled-faced and had black hair and mischievous eyes. He lived in the house behind Honey Bunch's. Norman and Honey Bunch, who were six years old, had no brothers or sisters, so the two children played together constantly.

"We might win first prize," Honey Bunch told her puppy, "but you'll have to stand up and laugh, Mr. Reilly."

Honey Bunch had named her dog Mr. Reilly for a jolly policeman who directed traffic on the corner not far from her home.

"Maybe we'd better give Mr. Reilly a rest," Honey Bunch said. "Let's see how everything else for the float is coming along."

The little girl's real name was Gertrude Marian but she was never called Gertrude Marian—just Honey Bunch. She skipped off, singing:

"Hi diddle diddle!
The cat and the fiddle
The cow jumped over the moon;
The little dog laughed
To see such sport
And the dish ran away with the spoon."

2

Honey Bunch and Norman walked over to see "the spoon that the dish was to run away with." Kitty and Cora Williams were working with Johnny Dale to make a large one. Cora and Johnny were holding up a piece of brown cardboard on which the spoon had been drawn. Kitty was trying to cut it out with a big pair of scissors.

"It certainly looks real," Honey Bunch said.

"But my hand hurts," Kitty replied. "Johnny, it's your turn to cut."

Mr. Reilly ran over and followed Honey Bunch and Norman across the yard. Here Ida Camp and Grace Winters were drawing a picture on a big piece of white cardboard. It showed a cow jumping over the moon.

"That's nifty!" said Norman. "Moo-oo-oo!"

"Thanks," said Ida, giggling. She brushed back a lock of her short, dark hair. "But I can't remember whether a cow's horns stick out forward or backward."

"I think it's forward," said Honey Bunch, who often went to her Cousin Stub's farm.

Near Ida stood Tommy Sand. Tommy was six years old too, and had light reddish hair and freckles. He was busy with hammer and nails putting a head, arms, and legs on an old wooden dish. Suddenly the hammer came down with a bang on his thumb.

"Ouch!" he cried, and danced around, sucking his thumb.

"Oh dear!" said Honey Bunch. "Come in the house and let me fix your thumb."

"Never mind," Tommy replied. After rubbing his thumb a few minutes, he declared it felt better.

Honey Bunch now decided to give her puppy another lesson. "Follow me, Mr. Reilly," she said.

The dog trotted after her under a big apple tree which was full of white blossoms. Back of it was a board fence which separated the Mortons' property from the Clarks'. Norman always climbed it when he came to play with Honey Bunch.

"Now stand up and walk!" the little girl told her puppy, lifting the dog's front paws.

Mr. Reilly's deep brown eyes looked lovingly into Honey Bunch's face, and he wriggled his black nose. But he did not move his feet.

"Oh, please," she said. "You want to be one of the Hi-diddle-diddlers in the parade, don't you? Ready? One! Two! Three!"

Carefully the little girl let go of the dog's paws and Mr. Reilly timidly stood alone on his hind legs for a second, took two steps, then dropped down.

"Goody! Goody! He did it!" Honey Bunch cried out, clapping her hands gleefully.

"Nice work, Mr. Reilly!" Norman said.

Honey Bunch patted the puppy's head and asked him please to repeat the trick. This time when she let go of his paws Mr. Reilly stood on his hind legs a few seconds longer. He took four steps. All the children gathered around

to watch him perform.

"I knew he could do it," said Norman. "Police dog puppies are smart, just like real policemen."

Mr. Reilly seemed as delighted as the children over his new trick. Suddenly, even without being told to, he stood up on his hind legs and walked around.

5

"Now we can have the best float in the parade!" Norman exclaimed.

"But don't forget," Honey Bunch said, "Mr. Reilly still hasn't smiled."

"Oh, I can make him smile," Norman declared.

"How?" Johnny Dale asked.

Norman did not answer. He leaned forward, put one hand in the air and the other to his mouth. "Whow! Whow! Whow! Whow!" he cried out, pretending to be an Indian.

As the puppy stared at Norman and cocked his ears, Kitty giggled. "You'll scare him instead of making him laugh!"

The little boy decided to try something quieter. He turned several somersaults. Then he stood in front of Mr. Reilly and made funny faces. Everyone laughed except the dog.

"I guess that won't work," Norman said finally. "Honey Bunch, what'll we do?"

"Paint a smile on his face," she replied.

Ida looked worried. "Won't that hurt him?"

"Not my kind of paint," said Honey Bunch. "I'll put on the smile with white cake icing."

"Oh, I'll bet he'll look funny," said Tommy.

Everyone except Ida thought the idea was worth trying. If a white smile could be frosted onto Mr. Reilly's face, then he would indeed look like the dog that "laughed to see such sport."

6

But Ida said, "I'm sure Mr. Reilly will lick it all off."

Nevertheless, Honey Bunch and Norman decided to try it out, and started for the kitchen of the Mortons' attractive two-story home. It was painted white and had dark red shutters.

"Mrs. Miller will help us," Honey Bunch said. She referred to a pleasant, middle-aged woman who helped Mrs. Morton with the laundry and other work and stayed with Honey Bunch when her parents were away from home. Mrs. Miller and the little girl were great friends. Mrs. Miller often used old-fashioned sayings which Honey Bunch repeated. But when the little girl said them, she usually twisted the words. This made the grownups laugh.

Mrs. Miller liked Norman too, but she thought he made too much noise. Now as the two excited children bounded into the kitchen, she said, "Goodness gracious, Norman, you don't have to slam the screen door so hard!"

"I'm sorry," Norman apologized. Then, to tease Mrs. Miller, he opened the door, put one hand to his lips, and closed the screen so silently there was not a sound. "I'm as quiet as a mouse hunting for some cake," he said, chuckling. "Mrs. Miller, will you make a smile for Mr. Reilly's face?"

"Make a smile for a dog's face? Now what kind of nonsense is that?" Mrs. Miller asked.

The children giggled, then Honey Bunch said, "We need some white icing so Mr. Reilly can be in the parade."

Mrs. Miller shook her head, saying she could not figure out this kind of "double talk." But when they finally explained so she could understand, Mrs. Miller laughed heartily.

"What will you two think of next!" she exclaimed.

She went for a box of confectioner's sugar and a bottle of milk.

"Honey Bunch," she said, "you're old enough to make the icing yourself and I have some work to do upstairs."

"Oh, may I?" the little girl asked eagerly. "How will I mix it?"

"Just put some sugar into a bowl," Mrs. Miller said, "and add a few drops of milk at a time. Keep stirring it until the icing is right for spreading."

Following Mrs. Miller's directions, Honey Bunch made a small amount.

"You know, Norman," she said, "a smile is like a good girl."

"What does that mean?" her playmate asked.

Honey Bunch was not entirely sure, but she said that it was one of Mrs. Miller's favorite sayings.

"But it doesn't mean anything," Norman insisted. "Why do you say it?"

Honey Bunch replied, "It's what Mrs. Miller

says when something almost doesn't happen."

"Oh," Norman said. "It sounds crazy."

In another minute Honey Bunch finished mixing the sugar and milk. "The smile's all ready," she said. "Let's try it on Mr. Reilly."

Norman opened the door for Honey Bunch and followed her outside. He whistled for the dog, who trotted up. All the children crowded around the back steps to watch the paint job.

"What'll we use for a brush?" Norman asked Honey Bunch as he held the dog still. "How about your thumb?"

But when Honey Bunch tried this, the icing fell off before it reached the puppy's upper lip.

"I'll get the squirt gun Mother uses when she puts icing on cake," Honey Bunch said and ran inside to get it.

Filling the pastry gun, she began to make a big white grin on Mr. Reilly. But it tickled the dog's lip so much he began to squirm. And as fast as Honey Bunch applied the frosting, Mr. Reilly licked it off.

"What'll you do in the parade, Honey Bunch?" asked Johnny. "He'll always lick off his smile."

Suddenly Honey Bunch thought of a way to settle this problem. "Remember the seals in the circus?" she asked. "They always get a fish to eat after doing their tricks."

"Sure," said Johnny, "but does Mr. Reilly like fish?"

"No, but maybe if we give him a piece of meat he won't eat his grin," Honey Bunch replied.

She went in to the refrigerator and brought out a few pieces of raw meat.

"Look, Mr. Reilly," she said, "this is for you if you're a good dog."

She held one of the pieces near the dog's nose and quickly squirted on another smile. Then, before Mr. Reilly could lick it off, she gave him the meat as a reward.

"Hurrah!" shouted Norman.

Just then Honey Bunch's lovely black cat, Lady Clare, came bounding over. Lady Clare was an aristocratic pussy with a white collar of fur. Usually she walked slowly with her head in the air, but now she jumped up and grabbed a piece of the meat from Honey Bunch's hand.

"You naughty girl!" Honey Bunch scolded.

Mr. Reilly growled, but the cat did not drop the meat. Instead she ran toward the apple tree, holding the piece between her teeth. The puppy wriggled free from Norman's grip and dashed after her. By this time Lady Clare had reached the tree and leaped up the trunk. Mr. Reilly barked at her angrily.

"Anyway," said Norman, "we know how to keep your pup smiling. And say, I'd better tend to my own job. I'm supposed to get the fiddle for 'the cat and the fiddle.'"

10

He ran to the back fence and climbed over to his own yard. In a few minutes the other children saw Norman coming back across the fence. In one hand he held a violin, in the other a bow.

"Hey, Johnny!" he called. "Come and catch this fiddle!"

As Johnny ran forward, Norman flipped the violin toward his friend's outstretched hands. But the instrument sailed past its mark.

"Ooh!" Honey Bunch exclaimed.

The violin hit a stone and cracked into two pieces!

CHAPTER II

A GREEN AND YELLOW FACE

THE BROKEN violin lay on the grass. It had snapped in two at the end of the neck, but the strings were still in place.

"Oh, Norman!" Honey Bunch cried, and Ida added, "What'll your mother say? Violins are very expensive."

"Not this one," Norman said, much to the relief of all the children.

He jumped down from the fence and picked up one piece in each hand. The little boy explained that it was a cheap instrument he had found in the Clarks' attic and which no one ever used.

"Anyway, I can fix it," he said. "Have you some glue, Honey Bunch?"

"I guess so," she answered and led her playmate into the kitchen.

Honey Bunch found a bottle of glue on a shelf and opened it. While she tipped the bottle, Norman smeared glue on the broken ends of the violin. But he got as much of the glue on his fingers as he did on the fiddle!

Now Norman pressed the two pieces firmly together. "There," he said, holding the fiddle very tight for a few minutes, "this'll never come apart again. Take it, will you, Honey Bunch, while I wash my hands?"

But when she took hold of it, Norman's fingers could not let go! *He was stuck fast to the violin!*

13

Honey Bunch began to giggle, but Norman wailed, "What'll I do?"

"You'll have to go around the rest of your life stuck to a fiddle," his playmate teased.

Norman did not think this was very funny and called loudly for Mrs. Miller. She came running downstairs.

"Are you in trouble again?" she asked.

Then she took Norman to the sink and held first one, then the other of his hands under the warm water faucet until the glue was washed away. Unfortunately the violin came apart too, so Mrs. Miller had to reglue it.

"Thank you," said Norman, and the two children hurried out to the backyard with the repaired violin.

By this time Lady Clare had come down from the apple tree and Mr. Reilly had forgiven her for stealing his meat. Honey Bunch had given him the last two pieces.

Norman laid the violin on the grass, picked up the cat and set her on top of it. Lady Clare remained very still.

"Wonderful!" Honey Bunch said. "Now all we have left to do on the scenery is paint the cow jumping over the moon."

The girls went to work with three paint-box sets to color the sketch on the cardboard.

"I'll do the head and the horns," Honey Bunch offered.

While the girls were busy painting, Norman shooed Lady Clare off the violin and held it under his chin. Picking up the bow from the grass, he shouted, "I'm a real fiddler!" He drew the bow over the out-of-tune strings, making a squeaky sound.

At this point Mrs. Miller appeared at the kitchen door. "Norman Clark, do you have to make that horrid noise?" she asked.

The little boy was sawing so loudly on the strings he could not hear her. Also, Norman did not watch where he was going. Suddenly he tripped over the dish which was to "run away with the spoon." He fell flat. His face landed squarely in one of the paint boxes.

"Ugh!" he cried, his nose in the green paint and his chin in the yellow. When he rose from the ground the other children howled with laughter.

"You look like a circus clown who got caught in the rain," Tommy told him.

Norman decided to go home immediately and wash. He laid his fiddle on the top step and raced for the fence. "I'll be back in a minute," he called.

It took Honey Bunch fifteen minutes to paint the cow's head brown and its horns gray. Norman had not yet returned and she wondered why. Laying down her brush, she said to the others:

15

"I'm going to Norman's house to see why he hasn't come back."

The little girl did not climb over the back fence as he had. Instead, she walked around the block and up the front steps of the Clark home. Norman's mother, a pretty, dark-haired woman, opened the door.

"Is Norman all right?" Honey Bunch asked.

"Yes, now that his face isn't every color of the rainbow." Mrs. Clark laughed.

"May I see him?" Honey Bunch requested.

"I don't think so, dear. Not right now, anyhow. Norman is practicing in the basement. He'll join you later."

Honey Bunch started down the steps, wondering what Norman was practicing. She tried to peer inside one of the basement windows, but it was covered with a curtain.

Now the little girl heard a humming sound coming from inside. What was Norman doing? She listened quietly for a moment. What could it be? Honey Bunch could not make out the strange noise. Shaking her head in puzzlement, Honey Bunch started home.

When she reached her own yard, Honey Bunch found that all the children had gone home. It was lunchtime.

"Why, I'm hungry, too," she told herself.

Just then Mrs. Morton drove in. Honey Bunch ran to hug her mother as she stepped

16

from the convertible. Honey Bunch looked very much like her slender, attractive mother.

"What a lot of work you've done this morning!" said Mrs. Morton, smiling. "And it looks very fine, too."

"Most everything's ready 'cept putting the things on the float," said Honey Bunch.

"What are you going to carry them on?" her mother asked, as they walked to the house.

"Norman's and Tommy's big coaster wagons," the little girl replied. "Tommy's father is going to put them together. He has lots of wood to do that."

When the float for the parade had first been planned, Mr. Sand had offered to help. He owned a lumberyard and would give the children boards to make a platform.

"Lunch is ready," said Mrs. Miller as Honey Bunch and her mother came into the kitchen.

After washing their hands, they sat down to the table, and Mrs. Miller served soup and chicken sandwiches. As she later brought homemade coconut ice cream, Norman walked in.

"Won't you sit down?" Mrs. Morton invited.

"Thank you," the little boy answered, and eyed the dessert.

Honey Bunch's mother smiled and said there was more coconut ice cream. "Would you like some?" she asked.

Norman said he had had his lunch but could eat two desserts any time.

"We had gingerbread cookies and I brought you one, Honey Bunch," he said, reaching into his pocket.

"That's nice, Norman," she said, then cocked her head inquiringly at the boy. "What were you practicing in your basement?"

"A big secret," Norman said. "I don't have to tell my secret, do I, Mrs. Morton?"

"Not unless you want to," Honey Bunch's mother said.

"Then may I change the subject?" Norman asked, repeating what he had heard his parents say.

"Of course."

As soon as Norman finished his ice cream, he said, "Honey Bunch, let's get the wagons ready for the float."

"Yes, let's," Honey Bunch answered eagerly, and everyone arose from the table.

The two children walked over to the Clarks' garage where Norman kept his coaster wagon. As they skipped up the driveway, the little girl noticed a glass jar set upside down in the middle of the yard.

"What's that for?" she asked.

"I caught a couple of bees this morning," Norman replied. "Would you like to see them?"

18

"Yes. But don't let them out. I wouldn't want to get stung! What kind are they?" Honey Bunch asked.

"Yellow jackets. They're yellow with black stripes."

The children approached the jar and lay flat on the lawn so they could look inside. The yellow jackets buzzed around for a while, then settled onto the grass.

"The poor things aren't getting enough air," Honey Bunch said. "They'll smother."

Norman snapped his fingers. "I have an idea!"

He got up and ran to the garage. A few

seconds later he returned with a shiny new bicycle pump and put the end of it under the jar. As Honey Bunch held the hose in place, Norman pumped air to the bees. The yellow jackets flew about wildly.

"Don't pump so hard, Norman," Honey Bunch cautioned. "You'll blow their wings off!"

Norman stopped pumping. "Keeping bees is an awful lot of bother. I guess I'll set 'em free."

As Norman raised one foot to kick over the jar, Honey Bunch cried out, "You'll get stung! I have another idea. Get a piece of string."

Norman ran to the house and brought back a handful of white cord. Honey Bunch carefully made a loop in one end and placed it over the jar. Then she trailed the string along the grass until both children reached the back door.

"You say, *'One-two-three-go,'* Norman, and I'll pull the string," Honey Bunch said. "When the bees get loose we'll run into your house so they can't sting us."

Norman declared the bees would not sting them. "They can't find us way over here," he said. He counted, *"One-two-three-go!"* Honey Bunch yanked the string and the jar fell over. Then she scooted inside the Clarks' kitchen.

But Norman did not follow her. "Ha, the

20

bees won't get me!" he boasted. "Look, they don't even know where I am."

At first the two yellow jackets hovered about the jar, flying in small circles. Then the circles grew larger and larger. Norman was fascinated as he watched.

"I told you they wouldn't sting me, Honey Bunch," he said, looking at her through the screen door.

Just then one of the yellow jackets made a dive for the boy. Before he could dodge, it lighted on his arm and stung him.

"Ouch!" Norman cried out and raced inside the house, howling for his mother.

She came hurrying into the kitchen. When Mrs. Clark saw the bite, she said, "The best thing for a bee sting is a coat of mud."

She took some dirt from a potted fern on a window sill and moistened it at the sink. Making a little mud cake, Mrs. Clark covered the bite. In a few minutes Norman felt better.

"If you're ready now," said Honey Bunch, "let's get your wagon. The bees have flown away."

Reminded of his job, the little boy went outside and brought his coaster wagon from the garage. The two children set off down the driveway. When they reached the sidewalk, Norman said:

"Hop in, Honey Bunch. I'll pull you."

His playmate climbed in and Norman stalked along manfully.

"Let's play taxicab," he suggested, starting to run. He made a *click-click* noise with his tongue like a cab meter, then said, "When the meter reaches five dollars, Honey Bunch, I think we'll be at Tommy Sand's house."

"It's already a dollar and twenty-five cents," Honey Bunch pretended with a giggle.

In a moment Norman decided to go faster. "I'd rather play I'm the pilot of a jet plane," he said.

The idea of going as fast as a plane appealed to Honey Bunch. "But don't go too high!" she warned.

Norman giggled. "Don't worry. I can always make a three-point landing."

He began to run very fast. Honey Bunch hung on tightly to the sides of the wagon, her blond hair blowing in the breeze. The wagon swayed.

"Please, not that fast, Norman," she begged.

The wagon was out of control! The next second the front wheels rolled against Norman's heels. He jumped out of the way, dropping the handle on the sidewalk.

Tiny sparks flew from the handle as it grated over the pavement. Suddenly the handle hit a crack. The coaster wagon jackknifed, and Honey Bunch sailed into the air!

CHAPTER III

A WIGGLY MIX-UP

Turning a complete flipflop, Honey Bunch landed on a green lawn to one side of the walk. The wagon banged into a small tree.

"Honey Bunch, are—are you hurt?" Norman cried out, as he ran over to his playmate.

"I—I guess not," Honey Bunch stammered, trying to hold back the tears. "I just hurt a little."

"I'm awful sorry," Norman said, as he helped her up. "Maybe we'd better go home."

"No, I'll be all right." The little girl dabbed a tiny handkerchief to her eyes and added, "Anyway, a smile is like a good girl," and gave Norman a big smile.

Norman put his wagon on the sidewalk again, and Honey Bunch climbed into it. "Please, no more jet pilot," she begged.

This time Norman pulled her slowly. In a few minutes they arrived at Tommy Sand's house. The little boy was waiting for them on his front porch steps. His coaster wagon was in the driveway.

"Guess what, kids!" Tommy cried out, as he dashed to the sidewalk. "We're going to the lumberyard in one of Dad's trucks!"

"That's swell!" Norman exclaimed.

Honey Bunch was pleased too. The children had never ridden in a big lumber truck.

A few minutes later a truck from Mr. Sand's yard drove up the street. It was an open-type truck, with an enclosed cab for the driver. The rear section had wooden slats around the sides.

As the truck stopped at the curb, a friendly driver opened the cab door. He stepped to the sidewalk and smiled.

"All ready to go?" he asked the children.

"Yes, Jack," Tommy replied.

Jack let down the tailgate of the truck and lifted the two little wagons inside. As he was closing the gate, Honey Bunch's puppy came racing down the street toward the children.

"Why, Mr. Reilly, you old runaway!" Honey Bunch scolded him. "You go right home!"

But the dog did not move. He sat down on

the sidewalk, looking hopefully at Honey Bunch as if to say, "Please take me too."

"He's a cute little fellow," the truck driver spoke up. "Why don't you give him a ride?"

"Will it be all right?" Honey Bunch asked Jack. "I'd love to take him."

"Sure thing," said Jack.

He let down the tailgate once more, and the puppy, barking happily, jumped into the rear of the truck. Norman followed, then Tommy climbed into the cab.

"May I ride in the back?" Honey Bunch asked.

"Up you go!" Jack said, and helped her in.

He locked the gate once more and went back to the cab. The motor started, and the truck rumbled slowly down the street. Mr. Reilly and the children peered out between the slats.

"Isn't this fun?" said Honey Bunch, as they neared a corner. "All the scenery looks different from up here. Oh!" she cried out.

A second later the truck's brakes screeched and the vehicle came to a sudden stop. The children were knocked helter-skelter.

Honey Bunch had seen a little boy dash into the middle of the street although there was a red light to warn him not to. The truck driver had jammed on his brakes just in time. Luckily, he had not hit the child.

Now there was loud whimpering from the rear of the truck. Norman's coaster wagon had been knocked forward and one wheel had run over Mr. Reilly's right hind paw.

Quickly Jack slid the back window of his cab open. "You kids all right?" he asked.

"Yes," Norman said, as they stood up, "but Mr. Reilly got hurt."

"Badly?" Jack asked.

Norman had moved the coaster wagon. Now Honey Bunch knelt to examine her pet's paw. There was a slight cut on it. When Mr. Reilly got up, he walked around on three legs. He refused to put the fourth one down.

"Oh, you poor puppy!" Honey Bunch said, hugging her pet.

Jack said he was sorry about the little accident. "We'll have the dog's foot taken care of as soon as we get to Mr. Sand's office."

Honey Bunch and Norman were very worried. Suppose Mr. Reilly was not able to be in the May Day parade! That would spoil everything!

The two children were very glum as the truck started again. Soon they reached the lumberyard, which stretched along the street for nearly a block. The office was at one end, just off the sidewalk.

Jack carried Mr. Reilly inside the office. Mr. Sand was not there, but his secretary, a pretty young woman, went for an antiseptic bandage for the dog's foot.

Mr. Reilly was very quiet as the bandage was taped on. But the instant he was free, the puppy pulled off the bandage with his teeth. Then he licked the cut. A moment later he stood up on all four legs and capered around as if nothing had happened to him!

"Oh, he's going to be all right," said Honey Bunch, clapping her hands. Then she hugged her pet.

Mr. Sand's secretary laughed. "Animals often know how to take care of themselves better than we can do it for them," she said.

Just then Mr. Sand walked in. He and Tommy looked very much alike. Smiling pleasantly, Mr. Sand asked, "Well, how are the Hi-diddle-diddlers coming along?"

Norman said that the float was almost ready.

"We just need the platform to go across the two wagons."

"We'll fix that for you in a jiffy," said Mr. Sand. "Let's go outside."

The three children trooped after him to the street. Jack had lifted down the wagons to the sidewalk. Now Norman and Tommy picked up the handles and walked along with Mr. Sand and Honey Bunch past the high stacks of lumber.

Tommy explained to his father about Mr. Reilly's foot. To everyone's surprise, the dog suddenly began to prance on his hind legs.

"That's great!" said Mr. Sand.

"Wait until you see his funny smile!" Norman boasted.

Just then Mr. Reilly dropped to all four feet and looked across the street. A man stood there staring at the dog. The stranger was slender and had stooped shoulders. He wore a dark green jacket.

"Does your dog know that man?" Mr. Sand asked Honey Bunch.

"I don't think so," she replied. "I've never seen him before."

At this moment the puppy lifted his upper lip, showing his teeth and his gums.

"Oh, look, Mr. Reilly's laughing!" Norman exclaimed.

"I wouldn't call that a laugh," said Mr. Sand.

"Honey Bunch, I think your dog doesn't like that man. Animals sense when people are not friendly to them."

"You mean the man doesn't like Mr. Reilly?" Honey Bunch was puzzled.

"It looks that way," said Tommy's father. "Well, let's get on with our job."

He turned down an aisle between the high piles of lumber, and soon they reached a carpentry shop. Inside a man in overalls was sawing a large board.

"Bill," said Tommy's father, "I want you to meet some of my son's friends. They're ready to have the platform put across their coaster wagons."

"And I'll be glad to help them," Bill said.

He smiled and showed the children a large piece of plywood which stood against the wall. He laid it across the top of the wagons, which stood side by side two feet apart.

"Will this be large enough for your platform?" he asked.

"Oh, yes, it's scrumptious," said Honey Bunch. Mrs. Miller always said this when she liked something.

"Are you going to leave it loose?" Norman spoke up.

"Oh, no," said Bill. "We'll fasten the platform."

From his workbench, he took a power drill

and bored two small holes in the bottom of each wagon. Next he put four holes in the plywood. Then he inserted bolts through the holes and tightened nuts onto them. The platform was secure.

"That's keen!" said Tommy admiringly.

Norman suddenly chuckled and a mischievous look came into his eyes. "Hey, kids," he said, "why is our platform like a railroad conductor's call?"

Honey Bunch and Tommy could not guess.

"Because it's *all a board,*" Norman replied.

The others laughed, and Bill said, "You're quite a joker, young fellow."

All this time Mr. Reilly had been lying on the floor. Now he arose and jumped onto the platform. The puppy seated himself in the middle of it and looked around. Everyone laughed.

"He's all ready for the parade," said Honey Bunch.

She thanked Bill for making the platform, and the children left. Jack was waiting for them and lifted the float into the truck. The children and Mr. Reilly climbed in and sat down on top of it. Two blocks from Honey Bunch's house Jack stopped.

"You children won't mind walking the rest of the way, will you?" he asked. "I must hurry off to pick up some lumber."

"Of course not," said Honey Bunch. "Thank you for the ride."

Jack helped them out, then took down the wagons with their platform.

"You'll go right to Honey Bunch's house, won't you, kids?" he requested.

"Oh, yes," the little girl replied. "We have a lot of work to do. The parade's tomorrow afternoon, you know. We have to decorate our float."

The children started off along the sidewalk. Norman and Tommy pulled the wagons while Honey Bunch walked in the rear. Mr. Reilly was perched in the center of the platform.

The wagon was so wide that a man and a woman who passed them had to go around into the street. But they smiled good-naturedly and did not seem to mind.

A couple of minutes later the children saw a boy coming toward them. He was carrying a fish pole over his shoulder, and in one hand was a pail.

"Say, what's the big idea of blocking the sidewalk?" he asked gruffly as he reached the children. "Move over!"

"But we can't!" Norman protested. "You go around."

The other boy took hold of the wagon handle which Norman was holding and yanked the float to one side. Mr. Reilly growled.

31

"You'd better leave us alone," Tommy warned.

"You think you're smart, don't you?" the boy sneered. "I'll fix you!"

With that, he put his hand into the pail. When he brought it out, his fingers held several worms. Quick as a wink he dropped them down inside Norman's shirt. Then the mean boy scooted off.

"Ugh!" Norman exclaimed, as the cold worms began to wriggle against his skin.

He wanted to run after the boy, but instead he reached down and grabbed the worms. Then he flung them onto the grass.

"That was a horrid trick," said Honey

Bunch. "But," she added, as the worms disappeared in the soil, "you did a good deed, Norman."

"How?" the little boy asked.

"You saved the poor little worms' lives," she told him. "If that boy hadn't thrown them at you, pretty soon they'd be in some fish's stomach."

This made Norman feel better, although he itched and said he would have to wash before helping to trim the float. When the children reached Honey Bunch's back yard, he went over the back fence and into his house.

By the time he returned, Honey Bunch and Tommy had started putting on the decorations. They had covered the platform with red and white crepe paper.

"That looks swell!" said Norman.

He helped them put red, white, and blue bunting around the edge of the float, so that the wheels of the coaster wagons would not show.

"Are we going to put the cow and the moon and the other things on the float today?" Tommy Sand asked.

Honey Bunch looked up at the sky. "I guess it won't rain tonight," she said. "Let's nail on everything now."

Norman giggled. "Mr. Reilly and Lady Clare won't like being nailed on," he teased.

Honey Bunch made a face at her playmate,

then got to work. The three children nailed
on the blocks of wood which held the cardboard displays. First the cow jumping over
the moon was fastened. Next came the big
wooden dish.

"And here's the spoon," said Tommy.

"You put that on while I attach the fiddle,"
said Honey Bunch.

As the children finished their work, Mrs.
Morton came from the house. "The float looks
marvelous!" she said.

"Do you think it will win a prize, Mrs. Morton?" Tommy asked hopefully.

"Perhaps."

Suddenly a strange look came over Norman's

34

face. "Prize winner," he muttered under his breath. Then suddenly he said aloud, "Goodby, everybody. I have something important to do at my house."

Without any further explanation, the little boy hurried off.

"It must be about his secret," said Honey Bunch. "I wonder what in the world the secret can be." She told Tommy about the funny noise in Norman's basement.

"I'm sure it has something to do with the parade," Tommy replied. "Norman told me yesterday that he was going to surprise us tomorrow."

All that evening Honey Bunch wondered what Norman's surprise was. She even thought about it as she lay in bed. Then she drifted off to sleep.

The next thing Honey Bunch knew there was a bright light flashing in her face. As she opened her eyes she heard a terrific crash outside. Then the little girl realized what it was —a thunderstorm!

Now she could hear the rain coming down hard and the wind blowing a gale. An awful thought came to Honey Bunch, and she sat straight up in bed.

"Our float!" she cried aloud. "Our beautiful float! It will be ruined!"

CHAPTER IV

A CURIOUS STRANGER

HONEY BUNCH hopped out of bed and dashed to her parents' bedroom.

"Daddy! Mother!" she wailed.

"What's the matter?" Daddy Morton asked, turning on a lamp. He reached out his arms and put them around his little daughter. "Did the storm scare you?"

"No," Honey Bunch answered, gazing at her handsome father. "It's my float. The rain will spoil everything!"

Mr. Morton smiled. "Well, I'm glad it's nothing worse that's worrying you. Honey Bunch, your float won't float away. I put it in the garage and closed the door. It's perfectly safe."

"Oh, thank you, Daddy," said the little girl

36

and hugged him hard. "Now the Hi-diddle-diddlers can be in the parade after all."

By this time Mrs. Morton was out of bed. She took Honey Bunch by the hand and led her back to her own room. Mrs. Morton kissed her little daughter and tucked her in for the second time that night.

The next day, which was Saturday, dawned bright and beautiful. It was a perfect one for the May Day parade.

During the morning the mother of each Hi-diddle-diddler was extra busy putting final touches on her child's costume. The outfits looked like the old-fashioned clothing worn by children pictured in nursery rhyme books.

"Mine is delicious!" Honey Bunch told her mother.

Mrs. Morton adjusted a little white peaked hat on her daughter's golden curls. Then Honey Bunch gazed at herself in a full-length mirror. Her long dress was the same shade of blue as her eyes. Over the skirt she wore a short white apron, and a pretty yellow scarf was draped around her shoulders.

Meanwhile, Mrs. Clark was having a difficult time with Norman. He said his outfit made him look like a sissy. The little boy wore short, purple velvet pants, and a blue, long-sleeved coat with a huge white collar.

"You look very nice, dear," Mrs. Clark assured him. She placed a high, wide-crowned purple hat on his head. In the center of the band was a large gold buckle.

"This hat's heavy, and it scratches," Norman complained.

"The other boys will be wearing them too," said Mrs. Clark. But she did put a soft handkerchief inside the hat, and Norman said it felt better.

By one o'clock all the Hi-diddle-diddlers had gathered in the Mortons' back yard. The little girls wore outfits similar to Honey Bunch's. Kitty Williams' dress was pink and Cora's yellow. Ida Camp's costume was pale green and very becoming.

"Hi, fellows!" Norman Clark said as Johnny Dale and Tommy Sand ran into the yard. He was happy to see that their outfits were like his.

Just before starting off for the parade, Honey Bunch made up another batch of white icing and carefully painted a friendly smile on Mr. Reilly's face. He did not lick it off because she kept feeding him meat. When the icing hardened, the puppy did not seem to mind having it on.

"Where's your brother Ned?" Norman asked Ida.

Ned, who was twelve, was to hold the two handles of the coaster wagons and pull the float. The girls were to walk one behind the other on

38

the left side and the boys on the right. Honey Bunch was to lead the girls and Norman the boys.

"My brother's coming in a minute," Ida replied. "Ned's putting on Daddy's old swallow-tail suit."

"Oh, I'll bet he'll look good in feathers," Honey Bunch whispered to Norman. "I like swallows."

The two children were surprised a few minutes later when Ned appeared. There was not a sign of a feather. He wore a black coat which was short in front and down to his ankles in the back.

"I thought you were going to wear feathers," Honey Bunch said.

At first Ned did not understand what she meant. But when he caught on, the boy started to laugh. "This coat is called a swallow-tail," he said, "because the tail in back is split, like a swallow's." He held up the two pieces.

"I see," said Honey Bunch, giggling at her mistake.

The swallow-tail coat was a little large for Ned, and the cuffs were turned under, but it made him look very dignified. With Mr. Morton's help he carefully pulled the float from the garage.

Everything was in place but the two animals. They would not be set on the float until the last minute. Honey Bunch picked up Lady Clare and Norman took Mr. Reilly on a leash.

"Here we go!" Ned called.

He pulled the float out of the driveway, with the other children following him. The Mortons, the Clarks, and Mrs. Miller waved.

"We'll see you later!" they called. "Good luck!"

As the Hi-diddle-diddlers walked toward the center of Barham, people on the sidewalk chuckled and praised them. Passengers in cars waved.

In a little while the children came to the town green where a high stand had been built. Flags were flying from poles on the corners. Several men who were to choose the winners stood on the platform.

"We'd better report to the Grand Marshal of the parade and find out where to go," said Ned.

"I see him," said Norman. "He has a big white badge. His name's Mr. Fitch."

He and Honey Bunch ran over to speak to the stout man, who also wore a "swallow-tail" coat. He had on a high hat. In one hand was a list of names.

"Your float will be number six," he told the children. "Please get in line on Beech Street. The parade will start there. When it's over, come back here and listen to the announcement of prizes."

40

Honey Bunch and Norman ran back to tell the others. Ned pulled the float around the corner to Beech Street and got in line.

What a crowd there was! And how attractive all the floats were!

First in line was a *Jack and the Bean Stalk* float. This was followed by one showing a pirates' den. Back of that was a funny float on which sat a *Humpty Dumpty* with a cardboard head fashioned like a large egg.

"Oh," giggled Honey Bunch, pointing to another float where she saw a girl she knew. "There's 'Mary' who was 'quite contrary.' Isn't she pretty with her cockle shells?"

"I'll say," agreed Ida. "She might win the prize!"

As the children watched excitedly, a band assembled at the head of the line. At a signal from the drum major, the musicians burst into a stirring march.

"*Rat-tat-tat! Rat-tat-tat!*" went the drums.

"We're going to start now!" Honey Bunch said. "Get in line."

She gently set Lady Clare alongside the fiddle. The music did not seem to bother the cat. She yawned contentedly and curled up against the violin.

Mr. Reilly was unleashed and put on the float. He moved about restlessly and would not stand up on his hind legs. His eyes darted

41

quickly from one side of the street to the other.
"Calm down!" Honey Bunch told him. She
reached over to stroke the dog. "Don't forget,

Mr. Reilly, you're the little dog that laughed.
When I say 'up,' please obey me."

Suddenly a whistle blew. The parade was
ready to go!

As the band began to play nursery tunes in
march time, Honey Bunch said, "Up, Mr.
Reilly! Stand up!"

The dog obeyed. He pranced around on his
hind legs better than he had ever done before.

"Good for you!" said Honey Bunch happily.

The icing smile painted on his face looked so
real that the crowds along the street curbs
laughed and clapped.

42

Mr. Reilly was behaving splendidly. He would prance awhile, then drop down for a rest. The children came closer and closer to the judges' stand.

"Look!" Honey Bunch suddenly called to Norman. "There's Elmer Gray." She looked toward a four-year-old boy on the curb. He was swinging a stick with a toy bird on the end. It fluttered back and forth, making a little whistling noise.

Elmer lived near Honey Bunch and Norman. Once in a while they played with him. He liked the castles they built in his sandbox.

"Hello, Elmer!" Honey Bunch called.

When the little boy saw her he dashed out to the float, waving his fluttery bird.

"Come back here!" Mrs. Gray called.

But Elmer paid no attention. Instead he took Honey Bunch's hand and marched along with her. Now the *Hi diddle diddle* float was only a few yards from the judges' stand. The men were looking at it and smiling.

Elmer became so excited that he twirled the toy bird faster and faster. Suddenly Lady Clare jumped off the violin and tried to catch it. Then with a great leap she landed on top of the moon. At once Mr. Reilly, who was on his hind legs, began barking and jumping up.

"Oh dear!" thought the Hi-diddle-diddlers. "Now everything's ruined!"

But the antics of the animals were so funny that the crowd burst into laughter. Even the judges chuckled to see the cat as well as the cow jump over the moon.

By this time Elmer's mother had run up to take her son away. Honey Bunch and Norman quickly calmed the cat and dog and put them back in their proper places. Everyone cheered, but the Hi-diddle-diddlers were sure they had lost their chance to win a prize.

"Tough luck," Norman called across to

Honey Bunch, after they had passed the judges' stand.

Suddenly the little girl noticed a man walking around the other side of the float toward Norman. He was the same slender, stooped man she had seen near the lumberyard— the man Mr. Reilly had not liked. He was again wearing his dark green jacket.

"I wonder who he is?" Honey Bunch thought.

The man bent down and whispered something in Norman's ear. The boy looked up, said something, then shook his head vigorously. The fellow frowned and whispered something again. Norman still shook his head. This time the man scowled and went back into the crowd.

"What did that man want?" Honey Bunch called over to Norman.

"He wanted to know who owns the trick dog. I told him you do. Then he wanted to know if you'd sell Mr. Reilly."

"I saw you tell him no," Honey Bunch said. "Norman, you were right. I wouldn't sell Mr. Reilly for anything in the world!"

Just then the Hi-diddle-diddlers saw their parents standing along the curb. They left the float to speak to them. Mr. Morton and Mr. Clark had motion picture cameras.

"We got some good pictures of all of you together," said Honey Bunch's daddy. "Now we'd like to get some of you alone. Go back a little way and skip toward us."

The two children did this as the cameras whirred.

"That was fine!" Mr. Morton said. "Now you and Norman had better catch up with your float."

The two playmates ran after Ned. He had parked the float along the curb and sat there mopping his brow. The cat was still resting on the fiddle. But the police dog was not in sight.

"Mr. Reilly," Honey Bunch called out, "where are you?"

Norman peeked under the float. "He's not there, Honey Bunch."

Both children called the puppy, and Honey Bunch gave a whistle he knew. Mr. Reilly did not come.

The little girl's eyes filled with tears. "Norman!" she cried. "Maybe that man took Mr. Reilly!"

CHAPTER V

CAUGHT IN A MAYPOLE

Had Mr. Reilly really been stolen? Ned Camp said he did not see how this could have happened.

"No one was near the float," he told Honey Bunch.

"Oh, I just know that mean man took my puppy," Honey Bunch said, tears in her eyes.

Norman felt very bad too. But he tried to console his playmate by saying, "The man said he wanted to *buy* Mr. Reilly."

"But he said he *had* to have a trick dog!" Honey Bunch reminded Norman. Now tears were running down her cheeks.

"Maybe Mr. Reilly got tired and went home," Ned suggested. "I'll go up to your house and find out."

"Oh, will you?" Honey Bunch said. She

dried her eyes. Maybe the puppy *had* gone home.

Ned started off. Just then the parents of Honey Bunch and Norman, who had heard the little girl crying, came over to find out what the trouble was. She told them, and Mrs. Morton bent down so her eyes were on a level with those of her small daughter.

"Please don't worry, dear," she said. "If Mr. Reilly isn't at home, we'll report everything to the police. They'll find your puppy."

"Oh, I hope so," the little girl said.

Honey Bunch's friends had come up. Ida said they should go to the square as Mr. Fitch, the Grand Marshal, had told them to do.

"Yes," Norman urged and started off. "Maybe we won the prize."

"Please come with me, Mother," said Honey Bunch, who still felt upset about her missing dog.

They walked to the corner and stood near the judges' stand. At that moment an announcement came over the loud-speaker that the judges were ready to name the winners. Honey Bunch and Norman and their friends stood very still to listen.

The mayor of Barham arose and went to the microphone at the edge of the platform. "I have the great honor of announcing the winner in the children's parade."

Honey Bunch squeezed her mother's hand very tightly as the mayor went on.

"First prize goes to—the *Hi diddle diddle* float, planned by Honey Bunch Morton and Norman Clark. And their friends who helped will get prizes, too."

Instantly a cheer went up and everybody clapped loudly.

"We won! We won!" Norman shouted, running over to Honey Bunch's side. He danced up and down like an Indian on the warpath until his mother made him stop.

Honey Bunch was both laughing and crying with happiness. *First prize!*

Again the mayor spoke. "And now will the winning float again parade before the judges' stand? Then we'll give the award."

"But Mr. Reilly isn't here!" Honey Bunch said, looking up at her mother.

"That's all right," Mrs. Morton replied. "The judges saw him on the float before, and they want to give you and Norman your prize."

"Ned isn't here either," said Norman. "What'll we do?"

But just then Ned Camp hurried up to the group. He said his father had driven him to Honey Bunch's house and back.

"Your dog is not there," Ned told the little girl, "and we didn't pass him along the way."

Honey Bunch felt like crying again. But

she knew she must be brave and not spoil the fun for the others. The little girl hurried off with the children to bring the float to the judges.

In the meantime the mayor announced second prize for *Mary, Mary, Quite Contrary,* and third to *Humpty Dumpty.* Then the band began to play *Hi diddle diddle.*

As the piece came to an end, the winning float pulled up. Everyone started to laugh. Instead of Mr. Reilly prancing and laughing, Norman Clark stood in his place. He grinned and made barking sounds.

"Oh my goodness!" said Mrs. Clark, as her husband chuckled.

The float was stopped directly in front of the judges' stand. Norman pawed the air like a puppy.

"Say, what happened to the real dog?" the mayor asked. Honey Bunch mounted the steps and told him.

"That's too bad!" the mayor said. He turned to the microphone. "Honey Bunch's pet dog, Mr. Reilly, has disappeared," he told the crowd. "Honey Bunch thinks he may have been stolen. Will you all please keep your eyes open for the police puppy? You'll remember him. He was the one with the painted-on smile."

There were murmurs in the crowd as the mayor went on, "If anybody finds Mr. Reilly, please return him to the Mortons' home on Grove Street."

Then he called Norman up to the judges' stand and presented the two children with a lovely silver cup.

"And in addition," the mayor said, "for you two and all your *Hi diddle diddle* friends, I have tickets to a performance of 'Peter Pan.' It will be coming to Barham in a couple of weeks."

"Thank you," said Honey Bunch and Norman together.

Honey Bunch took the tickets, and Norman carried the cup. They had just started down the steps, when an elderly woman hurried up to them.

"Maybe I can help you find your dog," she said. "I saw a man offer him some meat. The puppy jumped off the float to get it."

"Then what happened?" Honey Bunch asked excitedly.

"The man kept moving away, and the dog followed him. I didn't pay any more attention because I thought the puppy belonged to the man."

"What did the man look like?" Norman spoke up.

The woman said he was stoop-shouldered and wore a green coat. "I remember too, that his ears stuck out."

"He's the one!" Honey Bunch exclaimed. "He wanted Mr. Reilly. He *did* steal him!"

Mr. Morton had walked up in time to hear the story. "We must report this to the police right away," he said.

"I see a policeman!" Norman shouted, pointing.

A uniformed officer was crossing the square, and Mr. Morton hailed him. He told about Mr. Reilly and the strange man.

The policeman took a pad and pencil from his pocket and made some notes. "I'll report this to headquarters and also to the Animal Welfare League," he promised. "Don't worry, little girl. Your dog will be found."

Honey Bunch felt somewhat better. When a Maypole dance was announced, she said she would join it.

"Then let's hurry," Norman urged.

"Mother," said Honey Bunch, "will you take care of Lady Clare?"

"Yes, dear," Mrs. Morton replied, and the children hurried off.

The tall flagpole in the center of the green was to be used as the Maypole. At the top of it were fastened dozens of streamers in different colors. The red, blue, green, and white ribbons fluttered all the way to the ground.

"Each of you take a ribbon," called out a woman who was in charge.

All the children made a dash to pick up the ends of the streamers. Honey Bunch chose a yellow one. Norman was alongside her with a red one in his hand. When all the children were in place they formed a circle some distance from the pole.

The band struck up a lively tune and the dance began. Half the children in the circle were supposed to skip to the left and the others to the right, winding in and out as they passed one another. This would braid the streamers to the Maypole.

But what confusion! Some of the boys and girls got mixed up and went the wrong way. Three of them even stood still as the children who understood what they were doing tried to dance around them.

"Stop! Stop!" cried the woman who was leading them. "This is dreadful!"

Mrs. Clark asked the band to stop playing, and Mrs. Morton laughingly untangled the young dancers and their ribbons. Then she helped to place them in proper positions with a boy facing a girl all around the Maypole.

The directions were repeated by the leader. "Ready—" she called.

"Let 'er roll!" yelled Norman.

Again the band started. This time the dance went smoothly. Laughing and shouting, the children skipped in and out. The streamers began to make a lovely braid of many colors from the top of the Maypole.

After a couple of minutes, Norman became tired of just going round and round. He started to act silly. Holding the ribbon to the top of his head, he jumped up and down. Then he tried to climb the pole.

"Oh, Norman," said Honey Bunch as she passed him, "You'll spoil the Maypole's pigtails!"

Norman paid no attention and several other boys started to imitate him. The ribbon slipped out of Norman's hand and dangled toward the pole in the center. He ducked under the other children and tried to pick it up. The ribbon swished back and forth, out of reach.

"I'd better get that!" Norman told himself.

All this time he had not noticed what was happening to him. Tommy had given a wink to several other boys as they danced around. Now they began tying Norman to the maypole!

The ends of the ribbons were wound round

and round him. Before Norman realized it he was braided to the pole and could not free himself. The children all shouted gleefully.

"Help! Help!" Norman shouted. "I have to get out of here!"

Ida Camp skipped over and started to giggle.

"A boy with braids!" she teased. "Why don't you unbraid yourself?" But Norman's arms were pinned to his sides.

The little boy struggled to break the streamers but they held him tightly. "I *have* to get loose!" he cried. "I have something important to do!"

Suddenly a voice came over the loudspeaker. "Boys, get ready for the bicycle race!"

When Norman heard this he struggled furiously. "Get me out of here, Honey Bunch!" he begged. "The bicycle race—that's my secret!"

"Your *secret?*" she asked in surprise. Norman did not have a two-wheeler.

"Get these sissy ribbons off me," Norman begged, "and I'll tell you everything!"

CHAPTER VI

AN EXCITING RACE

"Now tell us your secret," Honey Bunch said, as she and Ida pulled the last streamers from around Norman.

"All right," he said. "I'm in the little boys' bicycle race. I didn't tell you because I wanted to surprise you."

"But you don't have a two-wheeler," Honey Bunch told him.

Norman grinned. "Sure I do," he said, throwing out his chest and looking very proud. "My father got me one. The bike's what you heard in my basement. I was riding it."

"That's fine," said Honey Bunch. She asked Norman why he had not ridden his new bicycle outdoors.

"My father wanted me to learn to ride well before taking my bike where there were other people," he explained. "I practiced real hard so I could be in the race and now I am. Well, I have to go."

"Where's your bike?" Honey Bunch asked.

"My dad's bringing it from our car."

The little boy started off. Just then another announcement was made over the loudspeaker. "There will be a slight delay in the small boys' bicycle race," the man said. "While we're waiting, we'll have a sack race for the little girls. It will be held in the center of the green."

"Come on, Honey Bunch, let's try it," Ida Camp said eagerly.

Honey Bunch held back. She was still worrying about her lost puppy and did not feel like playing the game. But Ida urged her to and took her friend by the hand.

"All right," said Honey Bunch and went along.

About twenty little girls gathered on the green. A young teacher named Miss Edwards walked forward to give them directions.

"This will be an unusual kind of sack race," she remarked, smiling.

Ida giggled. "Are we going to put the sacks over our heads instead of on our feet?" she asked.

Miss Edwards said Ida had come close to the

answer. Then she explained the game. "Besides having your feet in a sack, you'll be blindfolded with handkerchiefs."

"Then we won't know where we're going," said Kitty Williams.

Miss Edwards smiled. "That's the fun. But you'll hear music and try to find the player."

She pointed to the end of the race course, twenty-five yards away. A saxophone player from the band stood there.

Miss Edwards said that he would blow on his instrument and the children would head in the direction of the sound. The little girl who reached him first would win.

"Play the tune once," she called to the musician. He put the reed of the saxophone to his lips.

"Oh, it's *Yankee Doodle*," Honey Bunch said, taking a few marching steps.

At the end of the gay little song the musician added a *wah wah wah*. It sounded like somebody laughing, and all the little girls giggled.

"Now does everyone understand what she has to do?" Miss Edwards asked.

"Yes," Honey Bunch spoke up. "We find the Yankee Doodle man by his blowing."

Miss Edwards laughed and agreed. The girls put their feet into the sacks and the teacher tied a white blindfold on each child.

By this time a crowd had gathered to watch.

Several small boys, including Norman and Tommy, were on the sidelines to see the funny event. The musician began to play Yankee Doodle and Miss Edwards called out:

"One! Two! Three! Go!"

Honey Bunch began to hop like a rabbit. She could not see where she was going, but the music came loud and clear. The little boys urged them to hurry.

"Come on, Honey Bunch!"

"Faster, Grace!"

"You're gaining, Cora!"

The onlookers cheered wildly as the little girls hopped along, holding the sacks up to keep them from falling off.

"They look like a lot of grasshoppers!" Johnny Dale said, laughing loudly.

The sax player went through the tune once and ended with *wah wah wah*. Just then Norman saw the boy who had put the worms down his shirt. Norman felt like running across the green to give him a punch. But he did not want to interrupt the game.

Suddenly the strange boy cupped his hands to his mouth and went *wah wah wah* like the saxophone. At once half the girls in the race changed their direction and headed for the sidelines. The watching children began to jump up and down excitedly.

"Stop! You're going the wrong way!"

61

The musician instantly began to play again to lead the children toward him. Honey Bunch had turned for a moment. But now she knew someone was playing a joke. Quickly the little girl changed her course and hopped faster than ever.

"Honey Bunch is leading now!" Norman screamed.

"Ida is catching her!" Tommy shouted.

By now Honey Bunch was two hops in the lead. Six feet from the finish line Ida Camp tripped and rolled over, nearly knocking Honey Bunch down. But a moment later Miss Edwards called out:

"Honey Bunch wins!"

All the girls tore off their blindfolds and stepped out of the sacks. They praised Honey Bunch for her good race.

"This seems to be your big day," Miss Edwards said to her. "Here's your prize for winning the race."

She handed Honey Bunch a lovely bride doll. It wore a white satin dress, tiny high-heeled slippers, and a long veil.

"Oh, I just love bride dolls!" Honey Bunch exclaimed. "Thank you! Thank you!"

Her favorite doll was named Eleanor, and she played with her a lot. But Honey Bunch had recently admired a bride doll in a store window. She was thrilled to receive one.

By this time the boys' bicycle race was ready. Everyone hurried to the sidewalk to watch it.

"Line up at the end of the green," came the voice over the loudspeaker.

Norman had hurried to the spot, just ahead of Honey Bunch. The little boys were busy testing their bicycles.

"Hi, Dad!" Norman said. He skipped over to his father, who held a shiny red bicycle.

"Mount your wheels!" the announcer called.

There were seven boys in the race. They got astride their bicycles and put their feet on the pedals as the fathers held their sons upright.

"Once around the green," the announcer said,

"and give one another plenty of room. If any rider falls off, he's out of the race."

Several of the little contestants wobbled, and the starter had to wait until everybody was set, then he shouted:

"Go!"

Norman started well, but the boy on his right began to teeter in his direction.

"Look out, Norman!" Honey Bunch warned him. "You're going to be hit!"

Norman saw this just in time. He steered out of the way. But just then the lad on the other side of him came toward Norman.

Suddenly all three bicycles met and the riders went down in a tangle of arms and legs! The four other boys raced on down the green.

"Oh, Norman!" cried Honey Bunch. She felt very bad to think he was out of the race. And the accident had not been his fault!

Norman rose and brushed off his clothes. There were tears in his eyes as he wheeled his bicycle over to Honey Bunch's side. "I thought I could win the race," he said. "I didn't even have a chance!"

By this time the other boys still on bicycles were halfway around the course. Then suddenly a cry came from everyone who was looking on. As the four young riders went around a sharp turn, every one of them fell off!

Honey Bunch wondered what would happen now. Taking Norman's hand, she said, "You might still have a chance. Maybe they'll do it over."

The man in charge put a whistle to his lips and gave three long blasts on it. Everyone became quiet. "We'll run the race again," he called. "Everyone come to the starting line."

"Oh boy!" Norman shouted.

The young contestants returned. Once more the grownups held the bicycles steady. This time enough space was left between them so that if one went sideways, the rider would not knock his neighbor over.

"Ready! Set! Go!"

This time not one of the boys fell. All of them shot ahead at good speed. The onlookers cheered excitedly.

"Hurry, Norman, hurry!" Honey Bunch cried out.

65

When the little boy reached the first turn he was third. But here his practicing in the cellar gave him an advantage. Norman made the turn so well that it put him in second place.

Tommy Sand, who had received his two-wheeler the Christmas before, was in the lead. On the next turn Norman gained a few feet on Tommy. Now they were on the home stretch. The racers came nearer and nearer the finish line. The onlookers were jumping up and down.

"Go it! You're almost there!"

Now the boys were riding side by side. The pedals were going so fast they were like spinning pinwheels. Suddenly a man with a large gray sack under his arm ran from the crowd. He crossed the street right in front of Tommy and Norman.

"Oh!" exclaimed several boys and girls. They were sure there would be a crash.

But just in time the two little boys pulled to the side. The man disappeared among the people on the curb.

In turning Norman and Tommy nearly fell off their bicycles. But quickly they straightened them. A moment later the two boys crossed the finish line together.

"It's a tie! It's a tie!" several children shouted.

As the other contestants trailed in, Norman

and Tommy turned and rode back to the finish line. They wondered if they would have to race again to decide the winner. As they waited to hear about this, Norman looked around for Honey Bunch. In a moment she ran up.

Before she could say anything about the race, Norman whispered excitedly, "Did you see that man with the sack?"

"Not very well," Honey Bunch replied. "Why?"

"Listen," said Norman, "he's the one who wanted to buy Mr. Reilly!" Then he added breathlessly, "Maybe he had your pup in the sack!"

Just then the judge called out, "We have two winners—Norman Clark and Tommy Sand. Fellows, here's a prize for each of you."

As the crowd cheered he handed each of the boys an electric horn for his bicycle.

"Thanks a million!" said Norman.

"This is swell!" cried Tommy.

Both boys pressed the buttons. *Beep boop! Beep boop!* the horns went. Norman and Tommy grinned in delight.

All this time Honey Bunch had been clapping. She was glad the race had ended this way. But the little girl wanted to run after the man with the sack. She might get Mr. Reilly back!

Finally Honey Bunch interrupted her play-

mate's *beep-booping.* "Norman," she said,
"let's find that man!"

"What man?" Tommy asked.

"The one with the sack. Mr. Reilly might
be in it!"

Tommy stared at her. "That's right," he
said. "I heard a noise coming from the sack.
It might have been a dog whining!"

Honey Bunch started to run through the
crowd. The two boys stood their bicycles
against trees and asked Johnny Dale to watch
them. Then they dashed across the green after
Honey Bunch. Soon they caught up to her.

"I see that man!" she panted, pointing.
"Over there!"

The children ran even faster.

68

THE STRANGE man crossed the green. At the far side of it were a number of trees. In a moment he hurried among them and the children could not see him.

"Oh dear," said Honey Bunch.

By this time the children did not know which way to go. Norman asked a couple of boys standing near by if they had seen the man. The boys shook their heads.

"Look!" exclaimed Honey Bunch suddenly. "There's the first Mr. Reilly!"

Coming toward the children was a tall, good-looking policeman—the one after whom Honey Bunch had named her pet.

"Oh, Mr. Reilly!" the little girl cried out, grabbing the officer's hand. "Your namesake's gone!"

"What!" the policeman said. "You mean your dog ran away?"

"We don't know," Norman answered, "but we think a bad man took him and put him in a sack."

Honey Bunch told him the whole story and said some of the police knew about it. "But not about the sack," she said.

The officer patted the little girl on one shoulder. "I feel bad too about that namesake of mine being gone. He's a cute little fellow. We certainly must find him."

Policeman Reilly said he would start right away to hunt for the man with the sack. "And don't worry about the dog," the officer said. "Go back and have some fun."

The children hurried across the green. Norman and Tommy picked up their bicycles and thanked Johnny for guarding them. Then Honey Bunch and Norman went to look for their parents. They found them standing near a balloon seller. The children told them why they had run off.

"But Mr. Reilly number one is going to find Mr. Reilly number two," Honey Bunch said. Then, imitating Mrs. Miller, she said with a sigh, "It's a big load off my mind."

70

The grownups laughed, and Daddy Morton remarked, "I'm glad to hear that. I'm sure your pup will come home. And now, how would each of you children like a balloon?"

"Oh boy, would I!" Norman said excitedly. "Say, they're filled with gas!"

"May I have a red one, please?" Honey Bunch asked. "Red's my favorite balloon color."

"I like the green ones," Norman spoke up.

The balloon man smiled and said, "How would you like a special surprise I have today?"

From his pocket he pulled two funny-shaped balloons. One was red, the other green. He attached the red one to a small tank of gas he had on the sidewalk. *Hiss, hiss!* The balloon filled out here and there.

"A puppy!" Honey

Bunch squealed in delight. "And he looks like Mr. Reilly!"

Norman chuckled. "What's my surprise?" he asked.

The man tied a string onto the dog balloon and handed it to Honey Bunch. Then he attached the green balloon to the tank of gas. *Hiss, hiss, hiss!* The balloon grew large and fat, even bigger than the one Honey Bunch had.

"It's an elephant!" Norman shouted gleefully.

He took the balloon and jiggled the elephant up and down. Then he pretended to sit on it.

"I'm a circus rider," he said. "Howya! Howya!" he called.

Honey Bunch giggled. But Mrs. Clark warned Norman that if he became too rough with the elephant, it would certainly explode. So Norman stopped riding the balloon.

By this time the part of the May Day celebration for the grownups was starting. Honey Bunch and Norman said they would like to go home.

"I'll take them," offered Mrs. Miller, who had joined the group. She had been watching the children's parade with a friend. Later, at Mrs. Morton's request, she had taken Lady Clare home, then come back.

"You both did very well," she told the children.

"Thank you," said Honey Bunch. "But I'm kind of sad. Mr. Reilly is gone."

"I'm sorry to hear that," said Mrs. Miller, "but I'm sure the police will find him."

To cheer Honey Bunch up, Norman began to act silly. He took her dog balloon and barked. She smiled a little.

"What kind of noise does an elephant make?" she asked Mrs. Miller.

"Oh, he trumpets."

"Like this," said Norman. He gave such a horrible screech that Honey Bunch and Mrs. Miller clapped their hands over their ears.

When Mrs. Miller and the children reached the Mortons' back yard, Honey Bunch asked Norman to hold her balloon while she went inside to give Lady Clare her supper.

"Okay," Norman answered. "I'll play circus."

Honey Bunch filled Lady Clare's food bowl and the milk cup, but the cat would not eat or drink.

"What's the matter?" Honey Bunch asked her.

The cat walked all around the kitchen. Then she went through the other rooms on the first floor. Finally Lady Clare scooted up the front stairs. Honey Bunch followed her. The cat walked into each room, going under the beds and chairs. Then she went back to the first floor.

"I guess she's looking for Mr. Reilly," Honey Bunch told Mrs. Miller. "They always eat together."

The little girl picked up her pet and fondled her. "Don't worry," she said. "We'll find your playmate for you."

Just then Norman raced into the kitchen. "Honey Bunch," he called excitedly. "Come quick! Mr. Reilly's up in the apple tree!"

"Oh that's wonderful!" Honey Bunch cried.

She hurried out to the tree and looked up. The next moment she almost burst into tears.

"Oh, Norman, how could you play such a trick on me?" she exclaimed. "It's only the balloon that's up in the tree!"

Suddenly Norman

74

realized what he had done. "Oh, I'm sorry," he said. "I'll climb up and get the balloon. You catch the end of the string when I hand it down."

He tried to shin up the trunk, but it was too big around for his arms. So the children got a ladder which reached to the lowest branch. Norman climbed it and shinned the rest of the way to where the balloon was caught. He untangled the string. Honey Bunch climbed the ladder and grabbed the end of it.

At this moment the children heard a bell being rung at Norman's house. "My supper must be ready," he said. "See you tomorrow, Honey Bunch."

"Good-by," she called, as he went over the fence with his elephant balloon.

The next day was Sunday. Honey Bunch and Norman and their playmates went to church. After service they had dinner and then gathered in the Mortons' back yard. Norman and Honey Bunch showed the others their balloons.

"They're nifty," said Tommy. "Say, is Mr. Reilly back yet?"

Honey Bunch shook her head and said, "Maybe Mr. Reilly's in a hospital."

"A hospital!" Ida exclaimed.

"I mean an animal hospital," Honey Bunch explained. "If my puppy got hurt, that's where he'd go."

"That's right," Norman agreed.

"Let's find out," Honey Bunch urged. She ran into the house and asked Daddy Morton if he would drive her and Norman to Barham's two animal hospitals, and explained why.

"Yes, indeed," he said.

As the three rode out the driveway, Honey Bunch waved to her friends. "We'll be back soon," she called. "Wait for us."

Norman had taken the dog balloon and trailed it out the window. Once he almost lost it.

The first animal hospital Mr. Morton came to was called the *Bide-A-Wee*. He waited in the car while the children went inside. A young woman in a white uniform sat at a desk.

"May I speak to the dog doctor?" Honey Bunch asked her.

"He's busy, dear. Maybe I can help you," the woman said.

"Have you a police dog puppy here?" the little girl inquired.

The nurse opened a drawer and looked through a file of cards. "No," she said, "none of our patients happens to be a police dog."

Honey Bunch thanked her and the children went back to the car. Their next stop was at Dr. Harvey's Kennels. Norman carried the balloon in with him.

Dr. Harvey greeted the children and looked at the balloon. "Do you want me to give

76

the balloon dog some medicine?" he teased.

The children giggled. Then as Norman handed Honey Bunch her balloon, she asked, "Have you a real dog here who looks something like my balloon? His name is Mr. Reilly."

The doctor smiled. "No, I haven't." Then he added with a twinkle in his eyes, "I do have a dog that's called an *air*dale, but he's not full of air like your balloon dog."

As Honey Bunch and Norman laughed, they heard a loud yelp from the kennels in the rear. The veterinarian hurried off to see what the trouble was. Honey Bunch and Norman turned to leave.

Suddenly a large black dog rushed in through the open front door. Seeing the balloon, he jumped up to get it and nearly knocked Honey Bunch down.

"Get out!" Norman yelled at him.

The big dog kept on trying to reach the balloon. Honey Bunch let go of it and the red rubber dog sailed up to the ceiling. But the black dog caught the string in his teeth and ran around with it. He jerked and shook the balloon fiercely.

"Stop that!" Norman cried out.

He rushed at the dog and grabbed his collar with both hands. Honey Bunch held his head. The dog went round and round to get loose, but the children would not let go of him.

In a moment a woman dashed into the office. "Prince, what are you doing?" she said, and snapped a leash on his collar.

She told the children she was bringing him to the doctor's for an inoculation. Honey Bunch took her balloon, and the children left the kennels.

"Thank you for saving my air dog," Honey Bunch said to Norman.

Daddy Morton drove them home. He said he was sorry Honey Bunch had not found Mr. Reilly, but he was glad the dog was not in a hospital. When her playmates heard the story, they said the same thing.

"While you were gone," Ida spoke up, "we printed some signs to tack on trees."

"What kind?" Norman asked.

Grace held one up. It read:

PLEASE LOOK FOR MY POLICE PUPPY
CALL HIM MR. REILLY
HONEY BUNCH MORTON
GROVE STREET

"That's scrumptious!" said Honey Bunch.

"Let's tack the signs up right away," Norman suggested, and got a hammer and some tacks from the Mortons' garage. All the children set off with the posters.

"There's a good tree on the corner," Norman said when they reached the next cross-street.

A sign on it could be seen from two directions. Reaching up as high as he could, the little boy tacked one of the posters to the trunk of the tree.

"It looks good," said Grace Winters.

The children went on. Within an hour they had tacked several posters around town, then said good-by to one another. Honey Bunch promised to phone everyone if there was any news of Mr. Reilly.

PLEASE LOOK FOR
MY POLICE PUPPY
CALL HIM
MR. REILLY
HONEY BUNCH MORTON
GROVE STREET

But there was no news that evening nor the next morning. Honey Bunch was very sad.

"Try not to worry," said Mrs. Miller. "You know, things more often come out right than wrong. I always say, 'Every cloud has a silver lining.' That's sort of good luck."

"Well, I need it," said Honey Bunch, sighing.

Her mother had just walked into the kitchen. She smiled at Honey Bunch. "This time *I* have an idea," she said. "Suppose we put an ad in the lost and found column of tomorrow's paper."

She and Honey Bunch sat down to work on the advertisement. The little girl printed it carefully:

LOST: *Mr. Reilly, a police dog puppy. Please return to Honey Bunch Morton. Grove Street.*

Honey Bunch and her mother went downtown shortly after three o'clock. When they entered the newspaper office, Honey Bunch gave the paper to the clerk.

"Will this be in tomorrow?" she asked.

"Yes indeed," he answered. Then he added, "Today's paper is just off the press. Would you like to have one? Maybe somebody has found Mr. Reilly already and put an ad in the paper."

Mrs. Morton smiled. "Thank you. I'll look."

She opened the newspaper and read carefully.

"Why, my goodness!" she exclaimed, looking down at Honey Bunch. "It says here a police puppy has been found. He sounds very much like Mr. Reilly!"

"Where is he? Where is he?" Honey Bunch asked, jumping up and down excitedly.

"In the town of Pennhurst."

"Let's go get him!" Honey Bunch pleaded.

CHAPTER VIII

A SLIPPERY SLIDE

NEWS about a dog that looked like Mr. Reilly made Honey Bunch clap her hands. "Please, Mother, let's drive to that place right away."

"All right, but Pennhurst is an hour's ride from here," Mrs. Morton said. "Let's ask Daddy to go with us."

"Oh, yes," said Honey Bunch. "And Norman too."

Her mother nodded and replied, "We'll have an early supper and go after we eat. Norman had better eat with us."

"Goody," said Honey Bunch. "And Mother,

let's have two desserts—one at home and one at an ice cream stand."

"All right," Mrs. Morton agreed.

When Honey Bunch arrived home, she stopped in the kitchen to speak to Mrs. Miller. "Maybe—just maybe—we're going to find Mr. Reilly," she said excitedly, and told the woman about the trip they were going to make to Pennhurst.

Mrs. Miller nodded. "Finding Mr. Reilly is as hard as finding a needle in a haystack," she said. "Well, I hope you get your pup back. I sure miss him."

Honey Bunch now ran to the back fence and called loudly for Norman. In a few seconds he climbed over.

"We're going to go look for Mr. Reilly," she said. "The newspaper says maybe he's been found!" She told him of the advertisement.

"That's keen!" said Norman. "May I go along?"

"Yes, and come for supper at five-thirty."

Norman ran to ask his mother's permission and to change his clothes. He returned to Honey Bunch's house in a few minutes.

The two children could hardly wait for Daddy Morton to drive home. He always blew his car horn when he was half a block away. This was a signal for Honey Bunch to race out and meet him.

"There it is!" Honey Bunch cried out suddenly. She waited until the car stopped in the back drive. Then as her tall, handsome daddy stepped out of the car, she raced up to him.

"Hello," he said with a big smile and bent down to kiss her.

Honey Bunch flung her arms around his neck and hugged him tightly.

"My goodness," he said, unlocking her arms, "what's happened? Something very important, I know."

As he patted Norman on the shoulder, Honey Bunch told him about the ad. Daddy Morton said this was surprising news indeed.

Within an hour he and Mrs. Morton and the two children were on their way to Pennhurst. Honey Bunch and Norman rode in the back seat. They had been to Pennhurst many times, because it was on the way to the farm where Honey Bunch's cousin, Stub Morton, lived. Stub was a little girl who had been nicknamed Stub because she was always stubbing her toes.

In about forty minutes signs along the road began to point the way to Pennhurst. "We're nearly there," Daddy Morton said as he made a right-hand turn. "What was the address in the newspaper ad, Edith?"

Mrs. Morton took a clipping from her purse. "Fifty-six Walnut Street."

"This is Walnut Street!" Norman called out.

"And I see number 56!" exclaimed Honey Bunch a moment later. A sign on the lawn gave the name as Denton.

The house was an old-fashioned one with a large front porch. Seated on a glider was an elderly couple. Honey Bunch was first to dash out of the car with Norman following her. She ran up the porch steps, her blue eyes sparkling.

"Is Mr. Reilly here?" she asked.

The old lady smiled. "My, what a pretty little girl you are," she said, and added quickly, "I'm sorry but there's no gentleman here by the name of Mr. Reilly."

Honey Bunch was so eager to explain that her words tumbled over one another. "Mr. Reilly isn't a gentleman," she said. "He's a little boy—I mean a boy dog. He's my dog that was lost and you found him."

"Oh, the puppy we advertised about," Mr. Denton said. "Follow me. The dog's in a shed out back."

The children hurried with Mr. Denton around the side of the house and across a back yard full of flowers. At the rear was a shed.

"I've kept the pup locked up for fear he'd run away again before his owner could come for him," Mr. Denton said.

As they neared the woodshed scratching and whining sounds could be heard. The man opened the door and a young police dog bounded out. He wore a red collar with a bell on it. The puppy looked much like Honey Bunch's dog, but he was smaller.

"Oh!" she cried out, disappointed. "He's *not* Mr. Reilly."

Norman, too, was crestfallen. But just then the puppy jumped into Honey Bunch's arms, and she forgot her sorrow for a moment.

"You poor little lost doggie," she cooed sympathetically. "You're a sweetheart!"

Norman and Honey Bunch played with the puppy for a few minutes, then Mr. Denton put him back into the shed.

"Don't worry," he said to Honey Bunch. "I'm sure his owner will come to claim him. But I'm mighty sorry about Mr. Reilly. I hope you find him soon."

Honey Bunch and Norman sighed. They were more sure than ever now that Mr. Reilly had been stolen. They looked so sad that Mr. Denton wanted to make them feel better. He put one hand into his trousers pocket and pulled out a tiny, clear plastic ball with the figure of a man inside.

"Do you like puzzles?" he asked. "I made this one. Take it along and see if you can get the man's hat on his head."

Honey Bunch thanked Mr. Denton and ran to the car. She told her parents the puppy was not hers.

"That's too bad," said Daddy Morton. "But don't give up hope."

The children climbed in, and he headed the car back to Barham.

Honey Bunch and Norman began to work on the plastic puzzle ball. They jiggled and twisted it, but they could not get the hat on the man's head. Finally they asked Mrs. Morton to try it and handed the gadget to her.

Just then Mr. Morton pulled up to an open-air ice cream stand beside the road and stopped. A second later Mrs. Morton put the puzzle man's hat neatly on his head.

"Oh, Mother, you're wonderful!" said Honey Bunch. "How did you do it?"

Mrs. Morton chuckled. "No one could work this puzzle in a moving car," she said. "You children try it now."

She shook the gadget. Soon Honey Bunch, then Norman put the man's hat on.

Then everyone got out of the car and walked up to the ice cream stand. A sign on top of the stand announced that this was *Happy Harry's.*

The children skipped over to the counter, squirmed onto two stools, and began to spin around. Honey Bunch's daddy and mother joined them.

"Are you Happy Harry?" Honey Bunch asked a cheerful-looking fellow behind the counter.

"That I am," the man replied and gave her a big grin. "What will you have today?"

Honey Bunch said she would like pink ice cream. Norman wanted white.

"Then I'll have brown," Mrs. Morton said with a wink.

"Me, too." Her husband laughed.

Happy Harry picked up a large scoop and gave everybody double-dip ice cream cones; strawberry to Honey Bunch, vanilla to Norman and chocolate to the others.

"Ummm!" Norman said happily.

The two children soon tired of sitting on the stools. Norman jumped down first and said, "Come on, Honey Bunch, let's explore the woods out back."

"Okay." She followed him to a grove of trees. Under them were several picnic tables and benches, two fireplaces, and a children's slide.

"Oo-oo, let's go down it, Honey Bunch," said Norman, climbing the steps of the slide.

"You'd better eat your ice cream first," his playmate warned.

But Norman could not wait. Holding the cone in one hand, he cried out, "Look at me—I can do a trick."

Saying this, Norman got on the slide. But it was very slippery. As he stepped onto it, the little boy lost his balance and twisted around. He sat down hard.

The melting ice cream splashed into his face and onto his clothes!

Norman slid down backward and hit the ground with a bump.

Honey Bunch ran over to him. When she was sure he was not hurt, the little girl started to laugh. Her playmate was a funny sight with

88

blobs of ice cream all over his nose and cheeks.

"Guk!" Norman said, trying to wipe them from his face.

"I'll help you," said Honey Bunch.

She had a tiny handkerchief in her pocket and used this. It was soon soaked, so she looked around the picnic area for something else to wipe off Norman's shirt and jacket.

Under one of the picnic tables lay a gray sack. She crawled under to get it. When Honey Bunch picked up the sack she heard a faint jingling noise inside it.

"Maybe it's money," Honey Bunch told herself and thought, "This is just like the sack that man had."

She carried the sack to Norman, who was still seated on the ground. Honey Bunch held the sack upside down and shook it. Out fell a shiny object.

"It's a dog's license tag," said Norman.

Honey Bunch picked up the tag. "It's Mr. Reilly's!" she fairly shouted. "Oh, Norman, my puppy was in this sack! He *was* stolen!"

Mr. and Mrs. Morton had come to get the children and were as excited as Honey Bunch and Norman over the discovery.

"We'll ask Happy Harry about this," said Daddy Morton. All of them hurried to the counter.

"Happy, have you any idea how this sack got in your picnic grove?" Mr. Morton asked him.

The man thought for a moment. "Yes," he said, "a fellow stopped here in a red car last Saturday. Said he wanted to rest for a while in my picnic grove."

"And then what did he do?" Honey Bunch asked.

Happy Harry said he had noticed the fellow take a gray sack from his car. "When he opened it I was surprised to see a police dog puppy jump out," Harry said.

"Oh, that was *my* dog!" Honey Bunch said. "Where did the man take him?"

"*Your* dog?" Harry asked, amazed.

"He's Mr. Reilly, and that bad man stole him!"

Happy Harry whistled. "I'm sorry I didn't know about that or I would have nabbed the fellow. He snapped a leash on the dog's collar

90

and took him into the grove for a run. I got busy after that and didn't notice them until I saw the red car driving off."

Daddy Morton frowned. "The thief must have taken Mr. Reilly's license tag off and thrown it away with the sack."

"But where did he go?" Honey Bunch asked, her voice quivering.

Happy Harry shrugged his shoulders.

"Which way did his car head?" Norman put in.

"That way," Happy said, pointing up the road to the right.

"In the same direction as my Cousin Stub's farm," Honey Bunch told him.

Daddy Morton asked Happy Harry to describe the thief.

Harry thought a moment, then said, "As I remember, his ears stuck straight out!"

"Oh, he's the man from the parade," Honey Bunch said excitedly.

Happy Harry said he had noticed that the man had an out-of-state license on his car. But Harry could not recall the number. Daddy Morton thanked him for his information, then said they must leave.

During the excitement Norman's ice-cream covered clothes had been forgotten. Now Mrs. Morton noticed them and wiped Norman off as best she could with some paper napkins. Then the Mortons and Norman got into the car and drove off.

On the way home, Honey Bunch suggested that they stop at the Barham police station. "I want to tell Policeman Mr. Reilly about his namesake," she said.

When they reached the station house, all four went inside. Honey Bunch was pleased to find the officer there. He was just going off duty.

"Have you found your puppy yet?" he asked.

"No," said Honey Bunch, and told him what they had found out about the thief.

"This will be a big help," the policeman said. "I'll notify the state police right away, and they'll be on the lookout for the man."

Honey Bunch hoped they would find him, but she had had two big disappointments already. She did not want another!

The little girl left the police station with her parents and Norman. By the time they reached the Morton house, it was getting late. The sun was beginning to set.

Norman yawned. But suddenly the little boy closed his mouth and stared in amazement toward the front steps.

"Look!" he cried out.

CHAPTER IX

A FUNNY GHOST

HONEY BUNCH and Norman stared at the unusual sight. On the front steps of the Morton home sat two boys and two girls whom the children had never seen before. Each child was holding a police dog puppy!

"We found your dog!" they all called together, as Honey Bunch and Norman got out of the car and ran over. At once all the dogs started to bark. What a noise this made!

Honey Bunch glanced quickly from puppy to puppy. Not one of them was hers.

"Oh dear," she said. "None of these dogs is Mr. Reilly, but thanks for showing them to me."

The two girls and one of the boys got up from the steps and started to walk off. The dogs stopped barking.

The other boy hung back and frowned. Suddenly Honey Bunch and Norman recognized him. He was the boy who had thrown the worms at Norman.

"I want a reward," he said.

"But you didn't find my dog," Honey Bunch told him.

"You got to give me some money anyway," the boy insisted.

"She does not!" Norman declared.

He moved closer to him to defend Honey Bunch if the boy should become rough. Though Norman was shorter, he was not going to let this stop him!

At this moment Mrs. Morton came up and asked what the argument was about. The strange boy looked rather nervous. Then, without saying a word, he ran off.

Honey Bunch told her mother what he had said. "That wasn't right, was it?" the little girl asked, and Mrs. Morton answered, "No, it certainly wasn't."

Norman said good night and went home. But right after breakfast the next morning he decided to find out if Mr. Reilly was back. The little boy climbed the fence and called to his playmate. Honey Bunch came outside.

"Is your dog back?" Norman asked.

"No," Honey Bunch said sadly. "Oh, Norman, I hope the man who has Mr. Reilly is giving him good puppy food and being nice to him." A tear rolled down the little girl's cheek.

"Don't cry," said Norman. "What was it you told me about a good girl is like a smile?"

"That's right," Honey Bunch agreed and smiled at Norman.

"I'll swing you," he offered, not wanting her to feel sad. "Get on."

The swing hung from a large branch of the apple tree. Honey Bunch ran to it.

"I'll stand up and pump," Norman offered.

Honey Bunch sat down, tucking her skirt beneath her. Then Norman stood up on the swing in back of her and planted his feet on either side of the board seat. Back and forth they went, going higher and higher each time Norman bent his knees to pump.

"This is fun, Norman," said Honey Bunch. "You know, I just thought of something."

"What?"

"Maybe we ought to offer a reward for finding Mr. Reilly."

"Say, that's a *good* idea," Norman agreed.

He liked it so much that excitedly the little boy carried the swing higher than he should have. Suddenly it twisted.

"Ouch!" cried Honey Bunch as she got her

fingers pinched a little. Norman let the rope unwind.

"What kind of reward would you give?" he asked, pumping again, but not so hard.

"Ice cream cones, maybe. Two or three of them."

Norman thought Mr. Reilly was worth at least twenty ice cream cones.

"I guess you're right," Honey Bunch agreed. "But nobody could eat that many ice creams. We'd better think of something else."

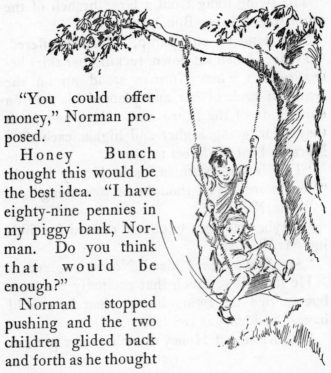

"You could offer money," Norman proposed.

Honey Bunch thought this would be the best idea. "I have eighty-nine pennies in my piggy bank, Norman. Do you think that would be enough?"

Norman stopped pushing and the two children glided back and forth as he thought about this. Finally he said, "Cowboys on television get a thousand dollars for capturing a train robber. Mr. Reilly's more valuable than a train robber. I think you'd have to offer two thousand dollars."

"Oh dear!" said Honey Bunch. She got off the swing and sat down on the edge of her sandbox. Norman followed her.

"I'd like to help you," he said, "but there's only a dollar in my bank. I guess you'll have to raise the money some other way."

"How?" Honey Bunch asked.

Norman wrinkled his brow in deep thought. Then he picked up a twig and began to trace funny faces in the soft sand.

"Come on, Norman," Honey Bunch prodded him. "How can we raise a big reward?"

Norman spoke of selling lemonade, but Honey Bunch reminded him that they had done this before and only earned fifty-one cents.

"Maybe we could build birdhouses and sell them," her playmate suggested.

"That would take too long," Honey Bunch reasoned. "Mr. Reilly would be a real old dog by that time."

"Don't *you* have any ideas?" Norman asked, his freckled nose almost touching Honey Bunch's.

"I've had an idea all along," Honey Bunch said impishly. "I just wondered whether you had the same one."

"What's that?"

"A show," the little girl replied.

"Oh, a puppet show," Norman said.

"No." Honey Bunch giggled and shook her head. "Oh, Norman, it's so simple you'd never guess. A movie show for children. But parents can come too."

Now her playmate was really interested. "That'll be keen," Norman said.

Honey Bunch outlined her plan. "We'll have a ride-in movie right here in my yard," she explained, "and charge everybody twenty-five cents."

The little girl had been with her parents to a drive-in theater outside of Barham. It would be exciting to have one herself for her friends.

Norman next asked about sound effects. Honey Bunch said that their show would have to be a silent movie.

"I could bring my record player," Norman offered, "and then we could have pretty music in the background."

"That would be good," Honey Bunch agreed.

The little boy asked what picture Honey Bunch would show.

She smiled. "The May Day movies your daddy and mine took. They'll be ready soon. Daddy said they might come back tomorrow. All the kids who had floats would love to see them."

"You're smart, Honey Bunch!" said Norman.

Honey Bunch giggled. "Let's see what my mother thinks about it."

The children hurried into the house. They found Mrs. Morton in the living room.

Mrs. Morton looked at the children, then said, "Your eyes tell me that something important is going on."

"Yes, there is, Mother," Honey Bunch answered. "Ride-in movies. To make money to get Mr. Reilly back. Please, may we?"

Mrs. Morton asked several questions about it, then said, "That's a very good idea. But don't worry about the reward money, Honey Bunch. Daddy will take care of that. How would it be if we give the proceeds of your show to the Barham Animal Welfare League?"

"Yes, let's," said Honey Bunch.

The children knew about this society. It sent sick dogs and cats to animal hospitals when their owners could not afford to pay for treatments.

Norman had been staring at Mrs. Morton. "You mean," he said, "that Mr. Morton is going to pay two thousand dollars reward?"

Honey Bunch's mother put an arm around the little boy. "My goodness, no," she said. "Whatever gave you that idea? Five dollars should be plenty."

Just then the front door bell rang. "It's the postman," Honey Bunch said. She hurried to open the door and took several letters and a package from the smiling man.

"Looks like some films for you," he said.

Honey Bunch thanked him and skipped back to her mother and Norman. "Part of our show is here," she said.

Norman started out the door. "I'll see if the postman has ours," he called.

In two minutes he returned, holding a package. "Here they are," he said. "Now we're all set for our ride-in movie."

"I'm afraid our movie screen won't be large enough," Mrs. Morton said, "if you expect a lot of children to watch the pictures."

"Can't we use a big sheet?" Norman asked.

"Very good, Norman," said Honey Bunch's mother. "We can hang it from one of the big branches of the old apple tree."

"My mother has an old sheet," Norman said. "I'll go get it right away."

He ran off but returned a few minutes later without it. "Mother is pressing the sheet," he reported. "She says there can't be a single little wrinkle in it or the pictures will look funny."

"Let's fix the entrance of our outdoor movie," Honey Bunch said.

The two children hastened to the street end of the driveway. They decided to set a couple of orange crates near the entrance. Someone would stand there and take tickets.

The children brought the crates from Honey Bunch's basement. They set them a few feet apart so that bicycles, tricycles, and coaster wagons would have room to pass through.

"And now we need tickets," Norman suggested. "What can we make them out of, Honey Bunch?"

The little girl thought hard for a minute. Then she said, "I have some 'old-maid' cards. They're nearly worn out from playing with them so much. We can write on the back of the cards and use them for tickets."

"Good! Get them, will you?"

Honey Bunch hurried to her room and opened the second drawer in her dresser. The cards were in the left-hand corner alongside some trinkets and a box of handkerchiefs. She also picked up her little fountain pen and hurried downstairs with the cards and the pen. Then the ticket-making started. On each card was printed:

RIDE-IN MOVIE
ADMISSION 25 CENTS

When the whole pack of cards was finished, Norman said, "Honey Bunch, do you suppose we can sell them all before lunchtime?"

His playmate thought they could. Norman

went for his two-wheeler and Honey Bunch pedaled her tricycle to the homes of their playmates. All the neighborhood children bought tickets, and the grownups too. They said they wanted to see the children's parade. In a short time most of the tickets had been sold.

"Hurrah! Hurrah!" cried Honey Bunch as the children pedaled home.

After Norman had his lunch he and Mrs. Clark carried the white sheet carefully over to the Mortons' yard. They laid it on the grass, then Mrs. Clark left, saying she had an appointment. Just then Lady Clare came from the house and started to walk across the sheet.

"Shoo!" cried Norman and grabbed her up. "Honey Bunch, we'd better hang this sheet on the tree right away before it gets all wrinkled and dirty."

Honey Bunch held the cat while Norman went to the garage for a stepladder. He dragged the folding ladder to the apple tree. Honey Bunch helped him set it up under the longest limb.

Norman wanted to nail the sheet to the tree. But Honey Bunch suggested that they tie strings to two ends of it and fasten them around the branch.

"Okay, I guess that's better," Norman agreed.

Honey Bunch took Lady Clare to the house and told her to stay inside. She found two pieces of string and hurried back to Norman.

After the children tied the strings to the sheet, Honey Bunch held up one side. Norman climbed the ladder, holding one string in his hand. First he tied the left side, then he came

down and moved the ladder. This time Honey Bunch went up and tied the other string.

"Are you sure it's tight enough?" Norman asked.

"I made knots and knots," she answered.

Honey Bunch came down and the children stood there a moment to admire their work. Then they carried the ladder to the garage.

While they were gone, little Elmer Gray wandered into the yard. At once he saw the sheet dangling from the apple tree.

"I can play cowboy and Indians with that," he thought, and reached for one end of the sheet. "This can be my tent. I'll take it to my back yard."

Elmer tugged at the edge of the sheet, and the string on the left side began to give. Then the one on the other side came off. Elmer pulled hard. The sheet fell to the ground, covering the little boy completely.

"Oh—oo!" cried Elmer.

Frightened, the little boy began to run with the sheet draped over him. At this moment Honey Bunch and Norman came from the garage. They stared in amazement.

"Our sheet's running down the driveway!" Honey Bunch exclaimed.

Norman giggled. "It's a ghost!"

They raced after the "ghost."

"It's Elmer," said Norman, recognizing the boy's shoes under the sheet.

"Oh!" screamed Honey Bunch suddenly. "Elmer's heading for the street. He can't see through the sheet, and a car's coming!"

CHAPTER X

POPCORN RAIN

"Look out, Elmer!" Honey Bunch cried.

"Come back here!" Norman yelled.

But Elmer, still wrapped in the sheet, seemed to be confused. He kept going. When he reached the curb, the little boy stumbled and fell headlong onto the pavement.

"Oh!" screamed Honey Bunch.

She and Norman began to wave wildly at the driver of the car coming down the street. Then they grabbed the sheeted Elmer and yanked him to the sidewalk.

The car stopped, and the driver got out. She looked upset and started to scold Honey Bunch and Norman for stepping off the curb.

"You must never run after toys that fall into

the street," the woman said. "Oh, my goodness!" she exclaimed, as Elmer's head peeked
out from under the sheet. "It's a child!"

"My name's Elmer Gray," said the boy.

The driver smiled apologetically at Honey
Bunch and Norman. "I take back what I said.
I'm glad you got Elmer out of the way in time.
What's he playing?"

Honey Bunch and Norman told her about
hanging up the sheet on the apple tree to show
movies of the May Day parade.

"We're selling tickets," said Norman.

"Please save me four seats," said the woman,
who told them her name was Mrs. Atkins. She
added that her children had also been in the
May Day parade and she knew they would like
to see the ride-in movie. "I'll pay for the tickets
at the gate."

Honey Bunch promised to save them, and
Mrs. Atkins added, "But tell me, what was Elmer doing wrapped in the movie screen?"

"He's a ghost," Norman answered.

"No, I'm not! I'm an Indian tent!" Elmer
declared, and told of his game.

Mrs. Atkins laughed, said good-by and drove
off. Honey Bunch and Norman unwound Elmer from the sheet, which was now torn and
dirty.

"I'm sorry," said Elmer.

"It's all right," Honey Bunch told him. "I'll

get a clean one. But we'd better not put it up till the last minute, Norman."

"You bet," he agreed.

"Please, can't I play tent with this dirty sheet? I'll bring it back later," Elmer asked.

"All right," said Norman.

He and Honey Bunch walked home with the little boy and helped him set up the tent. Then they went to their own houses. A little later that afternoon Honey Bunch saw the newsboy delivering the Barham paper. She ran to get it and quickly carried the newspaper to her mother.

"Let's see our ad!" she said excitedly.

Mrs. Morton turned to the *Lost and Found* column and pointed out the item about Mr. Reilly.

"Mother, maybe we'll get an answer real soon!" Honey Bunch said hopefully. "Unless that bad man keeps Mr. Reilly locked up where nobody can see him."

Instead of going back outdoors, she got her bride doll and played in the living room so she could be near the telephone. As the afternoon wore on, no one called with information about the lost puppy.

"I'm afraid he's gone forever." Honey Bunch sighed sadly.

About five o'clock Norman came over to see if she had heard anything. He sat down alongside Honey Bunch on a couch near the hall phone.

"Too bad," he said.

Then Norman became very quiet. This was so unusual that Honey Bunch looked at him. She thought her playmate was wearing a secret sort of smile.

"You look as if a canary swallowed you," Honey Bunch told him. She recalled that Mrs. Miller used a saying like this for anybody who looked as if he had a secret.

"You mean *I* swallowed a canary."

"You did?" Honey Bunch teased. "Did it choke you?"

Norman looked astonished for a moment, then said, "Course it didn't. I didn't even swallow a canary."

"But you just said you did."

"You said a canary swallowed me, Honey Bunch," Norman explained. "But you meant that I swallowed a canary."

"But you said you didn't."

At this point Mrs. Miller appeared in the back hall. "For goodness sake, children," she said, "get things straight. Norman, Honey Bunch means that you look as pleased as a cat who has swallowed a canary."

"Well, you do look happy about something, Norman," said Honey Bunch. "Will you tell me what it is?"

"Sure. I have an idea how to raise extra money at the ride-in movie this evening. Three guesses."

"Give me a little clue," Honey Bunch begged.

"Okay," Norman replied. "In the regular movies you buy something on the way in. Then right in the middle of the picture it makes a crunchy noise and people say, 'Hush! I can't hear a thing!' "

Honey Bunch looked puzzled. She thought very hard for a minute, then exclaimed, "Oh, I know! Popcorn!"

"That's right. We could pop some and sell it at the entrance gates."

"Crates, you mean," Honey Bunch said, giggling. She liked Norman's idea. Her uncle Rand, Stub's father, had given her an electric corn popper for Christmas. She loved to use it.

"Let's make some popcorn now," said Honey Bunch and ran to the kitchen, calling, "Mrs. Miller!" But the woman was not there.

"I guess she'll be back soon," said Norman, looking around. "There's a bowl of flour on the counter. I'll bet she's making a cake."

Honey Bunch said they need not wait for Mrs. Miller. The little girl knew the corn popper was on the third shelf of one of the cabinets. She pointed it out.

"I'll get the popper for you," Norman offered. He pulled the kitchen stepladder over and stood on the top of it. But he could not reach the third shelf.

"I guess I'll have to climb up and get the popper," Norman said.

"You can do it," Honey Bunch told him. "Mrs. Miller says you're a monkey. But be careful!"

Norman stepped onto the first shelf and held onto the third with the tips of his fingers. As he reached in to grasp the handle of the corn popper, one foot slipped.

Norman started to fall. He managed to land on the counter without hurting himself. But he kicked the bowl of flour off the counter. The kitchen was filled with white dust!

"Dear, dear! What's going on?" exclaimed Mrs. Miller, who was just coming up from the cellar.

"It was all my fault," Norman told her.

"We're sorry, Mrs. Miller," said Honey Bunch. "We were only trying to help the Animal Welfare League."

Mrs. Miller raised her eyebrows. "The what?" she asked.

Honey Bunch explained about making extra money. Mrs. Miller nodded.

"I'll sweep up the flour," Norman offered, jumping down from the counter.

"Me, too," said Honey Bunch and went for a broom and dust pan.

Meanwhile, Mrs. Miller got the corn popper from the shelf. "Next time you want this, please call your mother or me," she said. "I'll get some popping corn and butter for you." She lifted down a box of corn and pointed to some soft butter she had set out for the cake. Meanwhile, Honey Bunch got some cellophane bags the Mortons used to put sandwiches in for a picnic.

"Let's get started," she said.

"Do you need any more help?" Mrs. Miller asked the children.

"No, thank you," Honey Bunch said politely.

Mrs. Miller returned to the basement, and Norman and Honey Bunch started their work. First they put the kernels inside the popper and fastened the lid. Then Honey Bunch plugged in the electric connection.

Norman jiggled the popper back and forth so that the kernels rattled in the pan. Then he gave Honey Bunch a turn.

"This is fun," she said, giggling.

Suddenly there came a *plop, plop, plop*.

"It's making popcorn!" Norman shouted. He took the handle from Honey Bunch and began shaking the pan furiously. The corn continued to pop, now faster than ever.

"It's done!" Norman announced excitedly. "Let's open the lid, Honey Bunch."

"No," his play-

mate said. "It isn't all popped, Norman."

"Sure it is," the boy insisted. With that he opened the top of the popper.

Only half of the kernels had burst open. Suddenly the other half began popping furiously. The white, fluffy kernels jumped high into the air and landed on the table, chairs, and floor.

"Oh!" cried Honey Bunch.

"It's raining popcorn!" Norman said as he tried to put the lid back on. But the corn was popping so fast and the pan was so hot he could not do this.

In a few moments the popping stopped and the children gathered up the clean white kernels into a bowl. The ones on the floor were thrown away.

"I'll butter this bowlful now," said Honey Bunch. "You make some more popcorn, Norman."

The little girl poured the soft butter over the hot popcorn and salted it. Then she put it in the cellophane bags.

The next three batches of popcorn turned out well. Norman did not open the popper until the last kernel was cooked. Just as the children decided they had packed enough bags of the popcorn, the front doorbell rang.

"Will you answer it, Honey Bunch?" Mrs. Morton called. "It's the mailman."

Honey Bunch ran to the front door and opened it. The mailman smiled at her. "There's a letter for you this time," he said.

"It's from my cousin Stub," she told him.

Mrs. Morton came downstairs, and Norman ran in from the kitchen. Honey Bunch asked her mother to help her read the letter.

Mrs. Morton smiled. "If Stub wrote it, I'm sure there aren't any big words in the letter. You can read it yourself."

Honey Bunch tore open the envelope and followed the printing with her forefinger. The letter said:

Dear Honey Bunch,

I shall come to visit you tomorrow. Mother will bring me. We can play together. I hope I can stay overnight with you.

> *Your loving cousin,*
> *Stub.*

Honey Bunch was so excited that she jumped up and down. "Oh, isn't that scrumptious! I just love Stub. Please Mother, may Stub stay?"

"Of course."

Norman looked pleased too. "Maybe I can tie her to a tree again," he said, "like I did last time."

"Don't you dare, Norman Clark!" said Honey Bunch. She reminded him that Stub

114

had been tied so tightly Mr. Morton had had to come to her rescue.

"All right," Norman said meekly. "I'll just play tag with Stub. Well, I'll see you later, Honey Bunch. I promised Tommy I'd ride my bike with him. But I'll be back in time to put up the new sheet."

He returned after supper. Honey Bunch had a sheet ready. This time Daddy Morton helped tie it securely to the apple tree branch.

"It's perfect," Honey Bunch said. "Come on, Norman, let's take our extra tickets to the crate gate."

While they did this, Honey Bunch's daddy carried out some porch chairs to the yard. These were for the grownups. Then he set up his projector on a table near the house.

Everything was ready when the first patrons arrived. They were Norman's parents, who paid Honey Bunch fifty cents and went back to greet the Mortons.

"Isn't this exciting!" Honey Bunch exclaimed as, a moment later, she watched Grace Winters roller-skate down the street toward her.

Tommy Sand came behind Grace on his bicycle while Johnny Dale arrived on a scooter. They bought tickets and rode in.

"Step right up, folks!" Norman cried importantly, "and see the greatest show on earth!"

"Two tickets, please," said Betty Smith, who

was pushing Elmer Gray in a stroller. Honey Bunch, thinking Elmer was too old for this, looked at them curiously.

"The stroller was Mrs. Gray's idea," Betty said with a chuckle, "after she heard about Elmer playing ghost with your screen. I'm getting a quarter for minding him."

Elmer's face grew red. "I'm not a ghost and I'm not a baby. I'm an Indian!" he declared.

"Then I'm your squaw mother," joked Betty, "so you'd better stay put."

As she wheeled the stroller up the driveway, Kitty and Cora Williams and Ida Camp rode up on tricycles. Then several adults arrived, among them Ida's parents.

"This is a grand idea, Honey Bunch," said

Mr. Camp. "Mrs. Camp and I missed the parade, so we're eager to see your pictures."

"I hope you like them," replied the little girl as she took their admission fee.

The other grownups behind the Camps also paid Honey Bunch and went into the back yard. Last to arrive was Mrs. Atkins, who had almost hit Elmer. She and her children took the tickets Honey Bunch had saved for them. Then Honey Bunch and Norman followed into the back yard.

It was filled with people. Mr. Morton and Mr. Clark were seated behind the projector.

Norman ran up to Mr. Morton. "Let's start!" he begged. "I can't wait to see the parade pictures."

"All right, Norman," said Mr. Morton.

"First, we have to put on our Yankee Doodle record," Honey Bunch reminded her playmate.

"That's right," said Norman, and ran up the porch steps to start the player he had placed there. In a moment the lively strains of the music filled the air. Then the motion picture machine began to hum.

Honey Bunch and Norman took seats on the steps as colors and images flashed onto the big sheet. Instantly all the children laughed.

"It's upside down!" Honey Bunch called out in dismay.

CHAPTER XI

MOVIE EXCITEMENT

CLICK!

Honey Bunch's daddy stopped the upside-down reel, then wound it back. He fixed the picture correctly on the reel and started it once more. This time the movie was right side up.

"Oh's!" and "Ah's!" went up from the spectators as they watched the colored pictures of the parade. All the floats looked beautiful, and the children were cute in their various costumes.

"Here comes our float!" Ida Camp called out, as she saw Ned pulling the coaster wagons.

Norman ran to the player and put on the Hi-diddle-diddle record. Then he came back to his playmate.

When Honey Bunch saw Mr. Reilly prancing about with the icing smile on his face, she stifled a little sob. Norman, seated beside her, whispered, "Don't worry. We'll find him somehow."

As the picture of the float passed by, everyone clapped.

"Look! There are Honey Bunch and Norman alone!" Kitty cried out.

The movie showed the two children walking away from the float. Honey Bunch recalled that it was about this time when Mr. Reilly had been stolen.

Suddenly she cried out, "Daddy, stop the picture!"

Startled, everyone looked toward the little girl. Mr. Morton quickly snapped off the machine.

"What's the matter, dear?" Mrs. Morton said, hurrying over to Honey Bunch's side.

"I think—I think I saw the bad man who stole Mr. Reilly!" Honey Bunch said excitedly. "Daddy, will you please turn the picture back a little and run it over again?"

"Of course."

Mr. Morton reversed the film and then started the scene again. His daughter waited eagerly.

"It's coming soon, Daddy," Honey Bunch said. "I'll say 'stop' when you get to the place."

Just after the picture showed Honey Bunch

119

and Norman turning their backs to the float and starting to walk toward Mr. Morton, Honey Bunch cried out, "Stop!"

Instantly the movie remained in place. "There—in the corner of the picture!" Honey Bunch pointed. "Do you see him?"

"I do! I do!" cried Norman.

A man was standing on the far side of the float coaxing Mr. Reilly to come off. *The fellow had a sack over one arm!*

"That's the thief all right," Norman agreed.

"Now we have a good picture of him to show the police," Mr. Clark spoke up.

"I'll call them," Daddy Morton said. "Norman, you explain to everyone why the picture is being held up."

The little boy ran to the apple tree and made the announcement. What excitement there was as everyone awaited the policemen! With this picture of the thief, they surely could catch him!

Ida Camp walked over to Honey Bunch, who was watching from the driveway for the police car. "Wouldn't this be a good time to sell your popcorn?" she asked.

"Yes, let's," Honey Bunch agreed. "Will you do it?"

"I'd love to, and I'll get my brother to help me," Ida offered.

Ned and Ida went to the porch and picked up two large baskets filled with the popcorn bags. Then they walked among the audience, calling out, "Popcorn for sale! Freshly roasted by Honey Bunch and Norman! Five cents a bag!"

At once everyone wanted some. Just as the last bag had been sold, a car pulled up in front of the Morton home. Two men stepped out. They were not wearing uniforms and the children thought they could not be policemen. But Honey Bunch and Norman ran to greet them anyway.

"I'm Detective Gross," said the taller of the two. "This is my partner, Detective Dunn."

Honey Bunch introduced herself and said, "And this is *my* partner, Norman Clark."

Norman grabbed Detective Gross's hand. "Come and see the picture of the bad man who took Mr. Reilly!" he cried.

Arriving in the back yard, the police officers met the children's parents. Then Mr. Morton turned on the movie machine.

"There's the man!" Honey Bunch cried out.

"That's an excellent shot of the thief," Detective Dunn remarked. "After your show is over, I'd like to borrow this film, Mr. Morton."

"Certainly."

"Do you think you can catch him and get Mr. Reilly back?" Honey Bunch asked.

Detective Gross said there was a good possibility of locating the thief. As for finding Mr. Reilly, however, that might be harder. The thief might have sold the dog or given him away.

This thought was a new worry for Honey Bunch. "Please do your best," she begged them.

Her daddy showed the rest of the movie. It was so interesting that all the boys and girls begged to see the film again. After it had been run a second time Mr. Morton rewound it, then handed the reel to Detective Dunn. The policemen went off.

Mr. Clark now showed the movie he had

taken. In a moment everyone was laughing. Norman's father, who was full of fun, had photographed several of the children before the parade began.

One shot showed Honey Bunch jumping up and down trying to make Mr. Reilly perform his tricks. Then came a closeup of Norman's face. His lips were puckered as he whistled a tune.

Ida Camp giggled. "It looks as if he wants to be kissed. Maybe by Honey Bunch," she said. Norman was glad it was dark, because his face grew very red as everyone laughed.

The next picture surprised Norman's mother. It showed her standing on the curb blowing up a green balloon for Elmer Gray. Mrs. Clark's eyes popped and her cheeks puffed out as she blew.

"You did it, Mother!" Norman cried out as Mrs. Clark finished, and everyone laughed.

Nearly every child watching the show saw himself at the parade. When the film was finished, everyone agreed the ride-in movie had been a great success.

"Let's have more of them," Tommy Sand called out.

Honey Bunch announced that she and Norman had taken in ten dollars for the Animal Welfare League.

"That's swell," said Ned.

The children called good night and one by one rode out of Honey Bunch's back yard. Then the grownups left, and finally Norman started for home with his parents. "See you and your cousin Stub tomorrow," he called to Honey Bunch.

The little girl went into the house and got ready for bed. As Mrs. Morton kissed her daughter good night, Honey Bunch said:

"Do you suppose Stub is still full of them?"

"Full of what, dear?"

"Antics. That's what Mrs. Miller says Stub has in her."

Mrs. Morton said she supposed Stub would always be full of mischief, no matter how old she grew.

"That's why she's such fun," said Honey Bunch, then fell asleep.

She awoke an hour later than usual next morning. In the hall below, her mother was saying to Daddy Morton, "Here they are now!"

"I'll say hello to them before I leave," he answered.

Honey Bunch was excited. Could Stub have arrived already? She hopped out of bed and quickly put on her slippers and a cherry-colored robe over her pajamas.

Honey Bunch hurried downstairs and onto the front porch. She was just in time to join her mother in greeting Stub and Aunt Carol.

"Hello!" cried Honey Bunch.

"Sleepyhead!" teased Stub, a six-year-old girl who had dark, close-cut hair. She gave Honey Bunch a hug.

"You're going to stay tonight and lots of nights," said Honey Bunch.

Stub's mother smiled. "That's very nice," she said, "especially for today. Last night I received word that friends are coming this afternoon. So I'll have to drive back as soon as I do an errand in Barham."

"That's why we started so early," Stub said and added with a twinkle, "We got up before the chickens, didn't we, Mother?"

"Yes, we did," Aunt Carol said and laughed.

Because they lived on a farm Stub was used to rising early. Often she joined her daddy as he went out to milk the cows and feed the live-stock in the morning.

"But Carol," said Honey Bunch's mother, holding the screen door open, "you'll stay long enough to have breakfast!"

"Oh boy!" exclaimed Stub. "A second breakfast!"

She dashed toward the hall, stubbed her toe on the door sill, and went *kerplunk!*

"Oh, Stub! You've ripped your dress!" her mother said, as the little girl jumped up.

"I'm sorry," said Stub. "I won't fall if I have my play shoes on."

125

"Since you may stay," said her mother, "go get your suitcase from the car, but *don't fall with it!*"

Stub and Honey Bunch went for the bag. They carried it upstairs without any accidents and Stub began to change her clothes while Honey Bunch dressed.

Whenever the two cousins visited, they always had to talk over the news first before they started playing. As Stub kicked off her dress-up shoes she hopped onto the bed.

"I've learned a new trick," she said. "Look!" She did a backward somersault, coming to rest on the pillow.

"Good! Look at my new one!" Honey Bunch said.

She stretched out on the floor. Then she

arched her back and walked around like an upside-down crab.

"That's hard," Stub said admiringly. "Can you stand on your head?"

"I can if you'll hold my feet."

Honey Bunch hopped onto the bed and put her head down. Then she threw her feet into the air. Stub grabbed for them, but her cousin's legs swayed wildly.

"Hold—still—please!" Stub said, reaching for her cousin's ankles.

Suddenly there was a thud as both girls rolled off the bed and landed on the floor. This brought both mothers hurrying up the stairs to investigate.

"We're okay," said Stub.

"Sure," said Honey Bunch. "We're only doing tricks."

After their mothers left the room, the girls finished dressing. As Stub pulled on a pair of shorts, she told her cousin about a little pig on the farm. "He got lost, and we can't find him."

"That's too bad," Honey Bunch said, and in turn sadly told about Mr. Reilly being stolen.

Looking excited, Stub said, "I saw a dog two days ago that looked just like him!"

"Where?" Honey Bunch asked.

"He was in a carnival Daddy took me to at Rosevale," Stub replied. "It was near our farm!"

"Tell me all about it, Stub," Honey Bunch begged. "The puppy might be Mr. Reilly!"

Stub said that the dog had given a show on a platform with his master. He had done several fancy tricks. When the audience had applauded, the man had put something white on the dog's mouth.

"It made him look as if he were smiling," she said.

"Then it *was* Mr. Reilly!" Honey Bunch exclaimed, and told Stub about the icing smile. "I'm sure that man did the same thing!" Then she asked, "What did the man look like?"

Stub thought a minute, then said, "I'm afraid I can't remember, Honey Bunch. If I'd known the puppy was Mr. Reilly, I'd have told a policeman. Oh, I'm so sorry—"

"Do you know the name of the carnival?" was Honey Bunch's next question.

"No, but Daddy would," Stub replied.

"Let's go down and tell our mothers!" Honey Bunch said.

The two little girls hurried downstairs, and Honey Bunch told them about the clue to where Mr. Reilly might be.

"I'll call Rand now," Stub's mother offered and went to the phone.

Honey Bunch was fidgety until her aunt returned. "Your uncle Rand will call back," Aunt Carol said. "He'll try to find out more about the carnival. It wasn't a regular carnival that travels from place to place."

"Then what was it?" Honey Bunch asked.

"It was a show put on by various entertainers living in the area of Rosevale. That's the county seat. And the show was like a fair."

"I see," said Honey Bunch.

Just as they were finishing breakfast, the phone rang. Uncle Rand was calling. He talked to his wife for several minutes, then hung up. She came back to the table to tell the others what he had learned.

"Rand checked with the mayor of Rosevale. The mayor said the trick dog's owner was named Louis Milton. But he gave no address when he offered to be in the show. And this is interesting. He disappeared after the first performance!"

"Probably Louis Milton isn't his right name," Honey Bunch's mother guessed. "It will be hard to find him."

"What'll we do now?" Honey Bunch said, thinking it was becoming very hard to be brave about her lost pet. "We just *have* to find Mr. Reilly!"

"How would you like to drive out to our place tomorrow and spend a few days?" Stub's mother suggested, putting her arms around Honey Bunch. "Maybe you can pick up the trail of Mr. Reilly."

"Oh, Aunt Carol, that would be scrumptious!" Honey Bunch said, kissing Stub's mother. "And please, may I bring Norman? He's a good detective."

"Certainly. We'd love to have him. How about it, Edith?"

"I'll be glad to bring the children."

Stub was thrilled with the idea. "We'll all play detective and find your puppy, Honey Bunch," she told her cousin.

After Aunt Carol had left, Honey Bunch's mother said that, since they were not going until the next day, Honey Bunch might have a party that afternoon for Stub.

Honey Bunch went at once to the telephone to ask her friends. Soon she had acceptances from many boys and girls in the neighborhood.

"Let's go over and ask Norman ourselves," she suggested to Stub. "Then we can invite him to your farm, too."

"Okay."

Hand in hand, the two little girls skipped around the block to Norman's house. He was thrilled to go to Stub's farm. And he said he would like to come to the party that afternoon, too.

The three children played together all morning in Norman's yard. Near lunchtime they saw Mrs. Morton drive up the street in her car. It was full of packages.

"I wonder what's in them," said Stub.

Honey Bunch smiled. "Prizes and games for the party," she answered.

"Oh boy, I hope I win one!" said Norman.

He was the first guest to arrive at the party, which started at three o'clock. He had on a white shirt and blue shorts.

Norman came into Honey Bunch's house by way of the kitchen. Mrs. Miller was just finishing spreading chocolate icing on some freshly baked cupcakes.

"Oh, please, I want one now," Norman said.

When the kindly woman nodded, he picked up a cake and took a large bite. The rest of it broke in half and in catching it, Norman let a blob of chocolate land on his shirt. He looked at the spot in dismay.

"I guess I'll have to go home and get a clean shirt," he said. "But then I'll miss some of the games." He looked as if he were going to cry.

"Wait a minute," Mrs. Miller spoke up. "Maybe I can wash the spot off. I should have put the icing on tighter!"

She took a paper towel, wet it, and rubbed the chocolate. In a moment the spot was gone.

"Oh, thank you," said Norman happily as he put the last piece of cake into his mouth.

He went into the living room. Honey Bunch and Stub were there. They looked very pretty in their fluffy dresses.

As soon as all of Honey Bunch and Norman's friends arrived, Honey Bunch said, "Let's play Pin-the-Tail-on-the-Donkey."

Tommy Sand and Norman fastened the cloth donkey to a drape hanging between the living room and dining room. Then Honey Bunch tied a blindfold on Stub. She whirled her cousin around three times and headed her toward the donkey.

As the little girl turned to the right the other children squealed excitedly. Just then Norman stooped to pick up a penny he had dropped. His back was toward Stub. Straight in his direction, the little girl came, her arm extended in front of her. The pin was only a foot away from Norman.

"Look out!" Honey Bunch cried as her playmates howled with excitement.

CHAPTER XII

A LOST HIDE-AND-SEEKER

JUST as Stub was about to stick him, Norman turned. Seeing the blindfolded girl, he jumped out of the way just in time.

"Whoa!" he cried out. "I'm not the donkey!"

The noise and laughter confused Stub so that she turned completely around. Instead of heading for the donkey, she went to the hall.

"You're getting colder and colder!" Honey Bunch warned her cousin, but Stub kept going straight ahead.

When she stopped she had pinned the tail on the screen door leading to the porch. How surprised she was as she tore off her blindfold. Stub giggled when she was told how close she had come to sticking Norman.

"Oh dear, why did I stop?" she said. "I could have pretended Norman was a doll."

Norman looked disgusted. "It's a good thing you didn't!"

Each child took a turn trying to pin the tail on the donkey. Tommy Sand came pretty close, but Grace Winters put the tail right where it belonged, and the other children cheered.

"You win the prize, Grace," Honey Bunch said, and handed her a box. It was wrapped in white tissue and tied with blue and white ribbon.

Her eyes dancing, Grace removed the wrapping and opened the box. "Oh!" she exclaimed. "How beautiful!"

Grace pulled out a shiny bracelet with two ballet dancers dangling from it. She slipped the bracelet over her wrist.

As the girls admired the cute piece of jewelry, Honey Bunch said, "Here's a prize for you, Stub."

"But I didn't win," her cousin protested.

"It's the booby prize," Honey Bunch told her, giggling.

She handed Stub a large box wrapped the same way. Stub removed the ribbon and paper. Suddenly the top of the box flew open.

"Eeek!" Stub screamed, as a funny-looking clown popped out.

"I thought you'd like a jack-in-the-box," her

cousin said. "You can scare your friends with it."

The boys looked on, hoping that they, too, could win prizes. When Honey Bunch announced that the next game would be dropping clothespins into a milk bottle from far above it the fellows clapped.

"The clothespins have to fall off the end of your nose," Honey Bunch told them.

"I'm going to win this game," Norman answered, taking a bottle.

"No, I am," Tommy said, setting one in front of him.

The contest started with the girls going first. Bang! Bang! Bang! Most of the clothespins hit the rim of the bottle or the floor. Occasionally one would fall inside. Stub got three in, the highest score for any of the girls.

Now it was the boys' turn. Tommy put five into his bottle. Norman, who wanted very much to win a prize, was the last to play the game. Very seriously he held a clothespin to the end of his nose, then took a steady aim to the bottle top.

Bang! It went in! In all, Norman dropped five clothespins into the bottle and had only one left. All the children became very quiet as Norman took aim. This would be the deciding pin. He let it fall—right into the bottle!

"Norman wins!" Honey Bunch cried out. "Congratulations!"

Her little neighbor hopped around first on one foot, then the other, crying, "Hurrah! Hurrah!"

"Norman's a noisy winner!" Stub kidded him.

Tommy Sand looked disappointed until Honey Bunch announced, "We have a boy's and a girl's prize, and they are both alike. Since Stub already has won a prize, her prize will go to Tommy."

Everybody clapped and thought this very fair. Honey Bunch handed the boys the boxes. They opened them eagerly.

Suddenly two jacks-in-the-box, larger than Stub's, popped up and hit the boys on their noses!

"Ow!" Norman and Tommy howled, and the other children laughed gleefully.

"This is a great party, Honey Bunch," Tommy said, and Norman agreed with him.

"Now we'll play the word game," Honey Bunch announced.

Since this party was in honor of her cousin Stub, everybody should try to see how many words they could make in fifteen minutes from the name, *Stub Morton*.

Honey Bunch passed out papers and pencils. "You can use any of the ten letters in Stub's first and last names to make word combinations," she instructed.

How quiet it became as the children started writing!

"Don't whisper or give your words away," Honey Bunch warned as she heard Grace mumbling.

Suddenly Norman asked Mrs. Morton, "Is there such a thing as a Tonobu?"

Mrs. Morton replied that she thought not. "Gee," Norman said, "it sounded like a jungle animal to me. This is a hard game."

"Oh, it's easy," said Ida, her forehead puckered with thought. "I'm getting lots of words." Norman looked embarrassed.

After fifteen minutes had passed, Honey Bunch's mother asked, "All finished?"

"One more minute," Kitty begged.

Finally Mrs. Morton announced the end of the game and said, "Now count up how many words you have, children, and put the number on your papers."

When all the slips had been turned in, Mrs. Morton announced the winner. "Cora Williams has the most," she said, smiling. "She has fifty words."

"Fifty!" exclaimed Norman, scratching his head. "I only got ten!"

"What were her words?" Grace asked with a sigh of admiration.

Mrs. Morton read the following list: "On, no, not, ton, to, too, tub, storm, bust, bus, button, but, bun, root, mob, moon, boot, stun, stunt, must, turn, runt, rust, soot, soon, nut, trust, most, sort, sum, son, sun, room, broom, or, burn, tot, mount, rub, rob, motor, run, born, onto, motto, sour, torn, roost, snub, and burnt."

Cora smiled happily and accepted the prize she had won. It was a small Spanish doll dressed in a red-and-black skirt, white blouse, and lace mantilla. Even the boys thought it was a very pretty prize.

"And now we're going to eat," said Honey Bunch. "Find places at the dining-room table for ice cream and cake."

"Look out for the icing," Norman called out. "It's loose!" The others laughed.

By five o'clock the party was over. The little guests thanked Honey Bunch and her mother and left for home. Norman stayed because he wanted to play games a little longer.

"How about hide-and-seek?" he asked the cousins.

"Yes, let's," said Stub.

Norman volunteered to be "it" and stood under the apple tree with his eyes closed and counted by fives to one hundred. While he was doing this, Honey Bunch and Stub scurried off in search of hiding places.

When Norman finished counting he whirled

around and called, "Ready or not, here I come!"

Tiptoeing quietly about the yard, Norman spied Honey Bunch hiding behind the garage door. Calling out her name, he raced to the tree and tagged it before she did.

Then he started searching for Stub. He looked into all the familiar outdoor places where the children had hidden other times. He could not find Stub.

Finally Norman whispered to Honey Bunch, "Where is she?"

"I don't know," his playmate replied. "But I wouldn't tell if I did."

Finally Norman grew impatient. "I give up, Stub. You can come in home free." When he did not hear her, he called loudly, "Come in, come in, wherever you are!"

But still the little girl did not appear. Honey Bunch looked a little concerned and joined in the search. The two children even looked in the basement but Stub was not there.

"Maybe she hid somewhere else in the house," Honey Bunch said. "Let's ask Mrs. Miller."

The two children went into the kitchen and Honey Bunch said, "Mrs. Miller, have you seen Stub?"

"Am I supposed to tell?" the kind woman asked with a smile.

Honey Bunch explained that Norman had given up and that Stub could come in home free.

"Well, if that's the case, I'll tell you," Mrs. Miller said. "I saw your cousin come in a moment ago and tiptoe upstairs."

Honey Bunch went to the stairs and called to Stub. No answer. Then she hurried up the steps herself, her feet making little thuds on the stair carpet.

Going straight to her own room, Honey Bunch looked inside. Her cousin Stub was stretched out on the bed fast asleep! Honey Bunch did not want to awaken her so she started to leave the room. But just then Norman began to pound on the piano, playing "Three Blind Mice" as loudly as he could.

This awoke Stub, who sat up. She rubbed her eyes. "I'm sorry I didn't finish the game, Honey Bunch," she said. "I was hiding in that little carton on the back porch. It hurt my neck so I came in to rest a minute."

Honey Bunch wondered how her cousin had ever managed to squeeze herself into the carton! She and Norman had never thought of looking there!

When Honey Bunch explained the come-home-free, the two girls hurried downstairs.

"Oh, Norman," Stub said, after explaining what happened, "I just had the most wonderful dream."

When he asked what it was, Stub replied she had dreamed Norman found Mr. Reilly.

"That's great," Norman said, looking pleased

with himself. "Honey Bunch, I'm going to be a hero."

"You're silly," Stub said. "It was only in my dream, Norman."

The boy insisted that even if it was only a dream, he still would be a hero if he found Mr. Reilly.

"Well, I guess you would," Honey Bunch agreed. "And please do it."

The three children went into the kitchen where Mrs. Miller was preparing supper. When she heard about the dream, she smiled and said:

"If you keep on wishing hard enough, the dream may come true."

Honey Bunch was pleased and encouraged to hear this, but still she sighed. "Oh, I hope that man is giving my puppy the right supper and not making him work too hard."

Soon the Mortons' supper was ready, and Norman went home. But an hour later, just as Honey Bunch and Stub walked out to the front lawn, he rounded the corner on his bicycle. He was riding on the sidewalk and going very fast. When he reached Honey Bunch's house he slammed on his brakes. They made a squeaky, wheezing noise which caused the girls to giggle.

"Do you want a ride on my bike, Stub?" Norman called to Honey Bunch's cousin.

"I've never ridden a two-wheeler," she answered, running up to him.

"But you ride your own horse," Honey Bunch reminded her. "That's harder than riding a bike."

"Yes, but Joey Boy doesn't have wheels," Stub said, wrinkling her freckled nose.

Norman said that Stub had a good sense of balance—provided she did not stub her toe. "Why don't you try it?" he coaxed.

"All right, then," Stub agreed.

While Norman and Honey Bunch held the bicycle, Stub got on. Then Norman gave her a good push and Stub began to pedal. At first she wobbled all over the sidewalk but soon gained her balance. Honey Bunch and Norman ran along beside her.

"You're doing fine!" Honey Bunch exclaimed.

Finally Stub, several feet ahead of them now, called back, "How do you stop this and get off, Norman?"

The boy had forgotten to show Stub how to make the bicycle stop. It was hard to explain about the coaster brake while he was running so far behind her.

Now she started wobbling again. Then suddenly Stub shot ahead as the bicycle started downhill.

It whizzed across the lawn of a house and headed straight toward a fence. Beside it a man was planting rose bushes. The ground around them was uneven and muddy.

"Look out!" Honey Bunch yelled to the man. Hearing the call, he turned around just in time to get out of the way of the bicycle. The front wheel sank into the wet earth. As Norman and Honey Bunch looked on in horror, Stub was tossed over the handlebars.

Flop! She landed in the mud!

CHAPTER XIII

NORMAN'S RESCUE RIDE

"UGH!" Stub cried out and picked herself up.

What a sight she was! Mud was splattered over her face, arms, and legs, and her pretty green dress.

"Did you hurt yourself?" Honey Bunch asked her, worried.

"N-not much," Stub replied. "But my forehead got a bump."

Norman looked at his new bicycle. A little tremble in his voice, he said, "My bike's a mess!"

Stub was nearly in tears. "I'm sorry, Norman."

The man who was planting rosebushes

145

seemed too surprised to speak. He stood gazing at the damage.

But his wife, who had heard the noise, hurried from the house. When she spied Stub, she exclaimed, "You poor little girl! Wait right here!"

She dashed back inside the house and returned with a large white towel.

"I'll clean you off," she told Stub.

"But—but you'll get your towel all dirty!" Stub protested.

"Don't worry about that," the woman said kindly and went to work.

Suddenly Honey Bunch gasped. "Look at my cousin's forehead!" It had begun to swell. There was a large "egg" on it.

"Well, you did have a spill," said the woman's husband, forgetting his annoyance. "I guess you couldn't help it. I thought at first you were just careless."

He went inside the house for a piece of ice. He put a few cubes in a white handkerchief and pressed them to Stub's forehead while Norman pulled his bicycle out of the rosebed.

"I'm all right now," Stub said bravely, "but I'd rather ride Joey Boy than your bicycle, Norman. My pony stops when I tell him."

Honey Bunch told the man and woman that she was sorry for the damage to their garden. "I'm sure my daddy will pay for it," she said.

By now the man was smiling. He said accidents will happen, especially to children. They should forget the whole thing.

By this time the woman had most of the mud wiped off Stub. The little girl thanked her, and the children left.

Norman pushed his muddy bicycle along the curb. He did not stop at Honey Bunch's house. Instead he said, "Good-night. See you tomorrow to go to the farm." Then he kept on around the block to where he lived.

When the little girls entered Honey Bunch's house, Mrs. Morton looked at Stub in alarm.

"Gracious, what happened?" she cried out.

After hearing their story, she said she was glad the accident was no worse and suggested that Stub take a bath. When she was clean again, Honey Bunch's mother put a little bandage on Stub's forehead. Then both girls went to bed.

"I have a surprise for you, Honey Bunch," Mrs. Morton said. "Daddy is driving with us tomorrow."

Meanwhile, over in the Clarks' garage, Norman was having a hard time trying to make his bicycle look new again. He was not able to do it, and a lump came into his throat as he tried to keep from crying.

"What's the trouble, son?" called his father, and Mr. Clark walked in.

Norman explained, and his dad said they would soon fix everything. First he straightened the handlebars. Then he got a can of instant-drying red paint and touched up a few nicks.

"Get that can of wax," Mr. Clark told his son. "You can shine up your bike with that."

Norman followed directions, and in half an hour his bicycle once more looked new! He went to bed happy.

Early next morning Honey Bunch phoned Norman. He was not awake yet, but Mrs. Clark said she would call him.

"Oh, never mind," said Honey Bunch. "I just wanted to tell him my daddy is going with us, and he wants to start at nine o'clock."

"I'll awaken Norman right away," said Mrs. Clark. "Don't worry. He'll be there with bells on."

But when Norman appeared at Honey Bunch's house at eight-thirty, the little boy was not wearing any bells. Honey Bunch suddenly laughed. She remembered that this was only a saying. Right now it meant Norman was all ready.

He had brought a suitcase and his bicycle. Norman went at once to speak to Mr. Morton, who was packing the car.

"May I please take my bike with me?" he asked him. "I might need it."

"If it will fit in the trunk, Norman."

He tried it and found that the bicycle would go in nicely, even with all the suitcases.

"That's swell, Mr. Morton," said Norman. "Thanks."

"All ready, everybody?" Mr. Morton called out.

Honey Bunch and her mother came from the house. The little girl gave her cat a hug, then handed Lady Clare to Mrs. Miller, who was going to take care of her.

"We'll bring Mr. Reilly back with us!" Honey Bunch promised them.

Mr. and Mrs. Morton got into the front seat of the car, while the girls and Norman occupied the rear one. The children knelt on the seat and waved to Mrs. Miller and Lady Clare from the rear window as the car drove off. Then all of them sat down.

As they rode along Honey Bunch and Stub decided to look out one side of the car while Norman watched the road on the other side. They were doing this in case Mr. Reilly had escaped and might be on his way home. Honey Bunch saw a rabbit hop into the brush alongside the road, but that was all.

Suddenly the car began to make a strange grinding sound. "Goodness, what's that?" Mrs. Morton asked her husband in alarm. "It sounds dreadful."

Honey Bunch's father looked perplexed and pulled the car over to the side of the road. "Engine trouble," he guessed, opening his door and getting out.

Daddy Morton added that they were only halfway to Stub's farm. And he was concerned because they had not passed a repair garage in several miles.

"What'll we do?" worried Honey Bunch.

Norman got out of the car and peered up the road. Then he called to Mr. Morton, "I think I see a garage!"

The boy said it was a little way up ahead. He could just make out the red-and-white gasoline sign near a bend in the road.

Mr. Morton, meanwhile, had lifted the hood of the car in an effort to find the trouble. He poked around here and there but could not locate the cause of the strange noise.

"Let me get the garage man for you," Norman volunteered. "I'll ride my bike up there. Please let me do it, Mr. Morton."

Honey Bunch's father thought this might be a good idea and save time besides. He opened the trunk of the car and lifted the two-wheeler to the road.

Norman felt very proud of his errand and told everyone that he would rescue them as quickly as possible. Then he got on the bicycle and started toward the garage, being careful to stay close to the side of the road. His black hair blew in the breeze as he pedaled swiftly along the highway.

Finally he came to the bend and pulled into the combination gas station and garage. The attendant was surprised to see such a small boy riding alone so far out in the country.

"What can I do for you, sonny?" the young man asked, smiling, as Norman hopped off his bicycle. "Want some gas or a tire job?"

"I want you to rescue us," Norman said. Then he told the man what had happened.

"I'll go back with you and see what I can do," the garage man offered.

He walked into the garage and backed out a little jeep.

"Want to ride with me?" he asked. Norman nodded, and the mechanic lifted the bicycle into the back of the jeep.

"Oh boy!" said Norman as he climbed up onto the seat beside the man. How important he felt on this rescue mission!

The jeep sped down the highway and before long pulled up beside Mr. Morton's car.

"This young fellow wants me to rescue you," the garage man said, smiling.

"He certainly is a helpful boy," Mrs. Morton praised the lad. "Thank you, Norman."

"It was nothing!" Norman replied modestly, and swelled with pride.

The garage man took a tool kit from the rear of the jeep. Then, after listening to the strange noise in the motor, he began working on it. Norman peered in with curiosity, and Honey Bunch asked, "Mr. Garage Man, how long will it take to fix Daddy's car?"

The fellow said he did not know exactly, but it would probably take half an hour anyway.

"Then Stub and I could take a walk while you're busy?"

"You'll have time for that," the mechanic said, smiling.

"May we go, Mother?" Honey Bunch asked. "Just up that little hill to look at the woods."

"All right, but don't get lost," Mrs. Morton warned them.

Holding hands, the cousins climbed a grassy bank alongside the road and walked across a broad field in which daisies were growing. They stopped to pick a few flowers, then continued on to the edge of the woods.

"Listen!" Honey Bunch said. "What do I hear?"

"Water," Stub answered. "There must be a stream somewhere near here."

"Let's go see," Honey Bunch suggested and led the way toward the sound. Entering the woods, she added, "Look at the pretty dogwood trees."

How sweet-smelling the air was! Violets, daffodils, and other spring flowers peeked from beneath the rocks as the cousins made their way toward the sound of the babbling water. Soon they came to a little brook which was wider than they could easily jump across.

"It's scrumptious here," Honey Bunch remarked.

"Let's sail leaf boats," Stub proposed.

She ran to a small sassafras tree and pulled off some broad leaves. Then she snapped a few small twigs and stuck them through the leaves like masts on a sailboat.

"Here," she said, handing Honey Bunch one of the little boats. "Let's have a race."

Stub took the other leaf, and both little girls placed them in the stream. Away the leaves went, bobbing up and down over the ripples.

The girls dashed along the bank of the brook to watch the race. Soon the boats reached a place where the stream was dammed up with small stones, making a little waterfall. The tiny leaf boats were now swirling about side by side. Suddenly they zipped over the waterfall and raced out of sight in the rapids below.

"A wreck at sea!" Stub announced.

"Oh dear," said Honey Bunch. "Now we'll never know who won."

Just then she noticed a movement in the little pool before them. Several small fish were swimming about in the clear water.

154

"Aren't they cute?" Honey Bunch exclaimed. "But why are they going round and round?"

"They're looking for food, I guess," said Stub.

"Let's feed them," Honey Bunch suggested. Then she added, "I wish we had some fish food or bread with us."

Stub laughed. "We don't need that. I'll find some worms."

"Where?"

"Under these rocks," her cousin said, pointing to some near the stream.

Tomboy Stub poked a stick under a flat rock and up-ended it. Beneath was a cricket which scampered away quickly.

"Here's a nice big rock," Honey Bunch said. "I'll turn it over."

She bent down and put both hands on the rock. With a big tug she overturned it.

"Oh, Stub, a snake!"

Honey Bunch backed up so fast that she ran into her cousin and both girls fell to the ground. When they picked themselves up, Stub advanced cautiously toward the rock.

"It's only a garter snake." Stub grabbed the snake near the head and held it up. "This snake couldn't hurt you."

Honey Bunch took it from Stub and set the snake on the ground. "Go back to your children," she ordered, and the snake slithered away.

After the girls had turned over several more rocks, they found two worms and picked them up.

"Here comes your lunch!" Stub cried.

She and Honey Bunch ran to the edge of the pool and threw the worms into the water. Suddenly two swirls appeared on the surface as fish rose to nibble the food.

Then above the babbling of the brook Honey Bunch heard a familiar whistle. "It's Daddy. Come on, Stub, we have to go back."

When they reached the car, the mechanic was wiping the grease from his hands on a cloth. "I think that does it, sir," he told Mr. Morton.

"Thank you," Honey Bunch's daddy said as he paid the man. "You've sure been a life-saver!"

Norman cocked his head and listened to the purring motor. "It sounds fine again," he said importantly, and added, "We mustn't forget my bike."

It was taken from the jeep and put back into the trunk compartment.

"All aboard for Stub's!" Mr. Morton said, and the children piled into the car.

Honey Bunch gave her bouquet of daisies to Mrs. Morton. "Oh, thank you, dear," her mother said. "They're lovely."

The rest of the trip did not seem so long as the first part had. Suddenly Stub cried out, "There's our farm!"

How pretty the place looked! A white house stood in a cluster of trees with a large barn and silo behind it. In the green, fertile pasture behind the barn a dozen cows munched contentedly.

In a near-by field a man on a tractor was plowing up row after row of rich, dark soil.

"That's Daddy!" Stub said.

As Mr. Morton turned down the lane leading to the house, he blew his horn. The front door opened and Stub's mother appeared holding baby David in her arms. The child had been named for Honey Bunch's father.

Daddy Morton stopped the car, and they all got out. There were hellos and kisses. Then Norman started to race off to try to get a ride on the tractor. Mrs. Morton called him back, saying he must change his clothes.

The two girls looked at baby David, who was cooing. "May I hug him?" Honey Bunch asked.

"Certainly, but not too hard," Aunt Carol warned, smiling at her little niece.

"Hi, David!" Honey Bunch said softly, as she took the baby in her arms. She gave him a gentle hug and kissed his forehead.

"Now it's my turn," said Stub.

Her mother turned to the visitors and said, "Edith, you'd better call your house right away. Mrs. Miller just phoned here and she sounded excited."

"Is something wrong?" Honey Bunch asked anxiously. She immediately thought of Lady Clare. Had her cat been hurt?

Aunt Carol looked at the little girl and hesitated a moment. Then she said, "Mrs. Miller didn't say what she wanted. Only that it's something about Mr. Reilly."

CHAPTER XIV

A FRIGHTENED PONY

HONEY BUNCH was so excited, she tugged at her mother's hand. "Let's phone Mrs. Miller right away and find out about Mr. Reilly," she begged.

"All right," Mrs. Morton agreed. She too was eager to hear about the missing dog.

They hurried into Stub's house, followed by the others, and put through the call. Honey Bunch's head was right next to her mother's.

When Mrs. Miller answered, Honey Bunch asked her excitedly, "What happened? Is my puppy back?"

"No, dear," the woman replied. "But we're on the trail of the thief. The Barham police used your daddy's movie of him. They found the man's picture in their rogues' gallery."

"What's a rogues' gallery?" Honey Bunch asked.

Mrs. Miller explained that it was a collection of photographs of people who had been in prison for disobeying the laws.

"The thief's name is Stanley Jackner. He also goes by the names of Jones and Milton," Mrs. Miller continued. "He has been caught before for stealing animals. He usually works around carnivals. But no one knows where he is right now."

Mrs. Miller said this was all she had to tell them, except that everything was all right at home. After she had hung up, Honey Bunch told the others what Mrs. Miller had said.

"Wow!" Norman exclaimed. "Now we have to find a man with three names!"

"Oh dear," Honey Bunch sighed. "I hope we can find him with one of his names."

Uncle Rand, who had come in, laughed and told Honey Bunch that he had a hunch they would soon find the thief. The farmer was a tall, well-built man with a ruddy complexion and humorous eyes.

Honey Bunch hugged him excitedly and said, "How do you know?"

Her uncle said that the police had told him a man who looked like the one in the movie and driving a red automobile had been seen in several towns near by. Stub's father went on, "So I'm sure he will be caught."

Norman suddenly remembered something he had once heard a policeman say. Now he remarked in a deep voice, "The trap is closing on that bad man."

"I certainly hope so," said Aunt Carol, smiling. "And now, Stub, how about your showing Honey Bunch and Norman our new animals?"

The three children ran outside and headed for the barn. There were usually new kittens and puppies at Stub's farm.

"First I'll show you my pony," Stub said proudly. "You'll love him."

In a moment they came face to face with the lovely pony which Stub had recently received from her daddy. He was a Shetland, reddish tan in color. The pony nuzzled his young mistress as she patted his neck.

"I'd rather ride you, Joey Boy, than a two-wheel bike," Stub said to tease Norman.

She led her pony out of the stall and put a brown leather saddle on his back.

"He's nifty!" Norman said admiringly. "May I play cowboy?"

Stub reminded Norman that ladies always had a turn first. "Here, you get on," she told Honey Bunch.

Her cousin had ridden ponies before and knew the correct way to mount Joey Boy. Approaching him from the left, she put her foot into the stirrup and swung herself into the saddle.

"Let's go," Honey Bunch said quietly to the pony, lifting the reins.

Joey Boy clomped out of the stable and circled the barnyard at a walk. Then the little girl nudged him gently with her knees and he began to trot.

"Oh, he's wonderful," said Honey Bunch.

After going around three times, the little girl noticed an impatient look on Norman's face. So she reined in and slid to the ground.

"Your turn, Norman," she said.

The boy hopped on. He immediately began to shout, "Yippee! Ki-yi!" and waved his right hand in the air.

Instead of trotting, Joey Boy stood still and looked back over his shoulder.

"Come on! Giddap!" Norman called out, but the pony stood still, flicking a fly from his back with his tail.

"Why won't he go?" Norman called to Stub.

"Because he doesn't like loud commands," the girl replied. "You have to talk to him quietly."

Norman made a soft clucking sound, and immediately Joey Boy set off.

As the little boy continued his ride, Stub ran into the house and returned with a carrot in her hand. Seeing it, Joey Boy walked over to his mistress and made a little whinnying noise.

"Say *please* again," Stub demanded, and this time Joey Boy whinnied louder.

Honey Bunch fed the pony the carrot a bite at a time. When he finished it, Joey Boy bobbed his head up and down as if to say, "Thank you."

Just then Stub spied a large black-and-white dog loping across a field toward the barn. "Oh dear," she said, "here comes that mean old Zookie."

Stub told Honey Bunch and Norman how the unfriendly dog, which lived on another farm, often came over to annoy her pony.

"You'd better get off, Norman, 'cause Joey Boy might bolt," Stub cautioned.

Norman slid from the saddle and said, "Where's this mean hound? I don't see him."

"Over there," Stub answered, pointing near the side of the barn.

Norman ran toward the animal, shouting, "Get away from here! Go home!"

Zookie flattened his ears and ran off, disappearing behind the silo. Then all was quiet.

"Thank you, Norman," Stub said and added, "You'll have time for another ride, Honey Bunch."

The little girl got into the saddle again and after she had ridden around several times her cousin said, "Daddy and I taught Joey Boy a trick."

"Show me," Honey Bunch said.

Stub called the pony to her and then commanded, "Down, Joey Boy!"

The pony bent his forelegs, holding the hind ones stiff.

"Isn't that cute? He's bowing!" Honey Bunch said. "I didn't know that Joey Boy was a trick—"

Before she could finish what she was going to say, the children saw Zookie come bounding toward the pony. The dog had only hidden behind the silo.

"Scat! Get out of here!" Norman ordered as he and Stub tried to chase the black-and-white dog away.

But they were not in time. Zookie growled and nipped at Joey Boy's hoofs. The pony began to buck and kick. This jounced Honey Bunch up and down, and she had a hard time holding on.

Norman looked around for something with which to chase the dog. He saw a stable broom and grabbed it.

"Go away, you bad dog!" he cried out, waving the broom in front of the animal.

Zookie thought Norman was going to hit him, so he ran away. The little boy went after him and did not stop until Zookie was across the field and on his way home.

When Norman returned, Honey Bunch thanked him. And Stub's mother, who had come to tell the children lunch was ready, said, "Norman, you're a brave boy. You probably saved Honey Bunch from a bad fall."

The little boy looked pleased. At lunch he was given an extra piece of cake for his bravery.

When everyone finished eating, Honey Bunch's daddy said he was going to town. "I want to talk to the police and other people about Mr. Reilly," he said. Mr. Morton smiled at his small daughter. "Maybe by tonight we'll know more about your missing puppy."

"Oh, Daddy, please try real hard to find Mr. Reilly," Honey Bunch begged, as she said good-by to him.

"I will if you'll promise not to worry this afternoon and have fun here with Stub and Norman," he told her.

"I promise, Daddy. A good little girl is like a smile." She went outside with Norman and Stub and together they walked to the barn.

"I know a good game," Norman said.

"What's that?" Stub asked.

"It's called *Find the Pig,*" he answered.

This made Honey Bunch and Stub giggle. "Who'll be the pig?" Stub asked.

"I will," Norman offered. "And I know a swell place to hide. Then I'll make a noise like a pig. See if you can find me."

The two girls waited outside the barn until they thought Norman had had time to hide himself. Then they went in.

Oink! Oink! Oink! Oink! The sounds came from the overhead haymow. The little girls started to climb up the ladder.

Suddenly the same kind of noise came from among the bales of hay on the first floor. *Oink! Oink! Oink!*

Honey Bunch looked perplexed. "How could Norman be in two places at once?" she asked Stub.

The girls stood very still and listened. *Oink! Oink!* came the sound again from above. Then came *oink oink oink* from the other spot. The girls were greatly puzzled. Was there an echo in the barn?

"Which place shall we look first?" Honey Bunch asked.

"Norman's probably on this floor," Stub whispered. "Let's find out!"

The cousins crept up on the spot like two kittens about to surprise a mouse. Suddenly Stub saw a slight movement in some loose hay and together the girls pounced on the spot.

"We've got you, Norman!" Honey Bunch cried out as there was a loud squeal from beneath.

As she and Stub pushed the straw aside, Honey Bunch

gave a shriek of surprise. Norman was not underneath. Instead there stood a real pig! "Oh!" she exclaimed.

"My lost baby pig!" Stub cried out happily.

She took the little pig up in her arms. Just then Norman popped his head over the loft edge to see what was going on. He stared for a moment, then said:

"Hey, you caught the wrong pig!"

The girls giggled and Stub said, "So you're a pig, eh? Come with me, Mr. Oink-oink Clark and I'll put you in the pen with your brother."

Norman blushed, but Honey Bunch laughed so hard that tears rolled down her cheeks. "Oh, shush!" Norman said. "Anyway, you didn't find me."

"You didn't give us a chance," Stub told him. "Come on down and we'll put this little pig in with his mother. He must be starved. He's been lost for nearly three days."

The pig did not look starved, however. The children finally decided that the pig must be able to squeeze under the pen fence, and come in and out as he pleased.

"I guess he goes back to his mommy for meals," said Stub. "The rest of the time he takes naps in the hay."

The three children took the pig back to the pen behind the silo. His mother seemed very happy to see her baby again, because she rubbed noses with him. Stub got a board and laid it lengthwise against the bottom of the pen so the baby pig could not get out again.

Honey Bunch smiled. "Now the little runaway won't worry his mommy any more."

By suppertime Honey Bunch's daddy had come back to the farm. He had news for the others.

"I learned this afternoon that there's to be a show tomorrow at Midville. It's about twenty miles from here. The show will be very much like the one you saw, Stub."

"And you think maybe Mr. Three Names will be there with Mr. Reilly?" Honey Bunch asked excitedly.

"It's just possible," Daddy Morton said. "Anyway, we'll go to Midville and find out."

The children were very excited to hear this. As they went to bed, they wondered if tomorrow would ever come!

"Wake up, curly locks!" Stub said, shaking her cousin the next morning. "I've been downstairs for hours."

"What's the matter?" Honey Bunch asked, sitting up and rubbing her eyes.

"Daddy wants to see you and Norman right away. It's important."

Honey Bunch put on her robe and slippers and hurried downstairs. Norman was already there. He was dressed.

"I'm sorry I slept so long, Uncle Rand," Honey Bunch apologized.

"It's only eight o'clock," he said, smiling and putting Honey Bunch on his knee. "Children, I've just had a phone call from the Midville police department. They're holding a man they believe is the one who stole Mr. Reilly."

"Hurrah!" shouted Norman. "The trap got the bad man!"

Honey Bunch was so happy she hugged her uncle extra hard. "And now I'll get my puppy back!"

Uncle Rand said the police wanted the children to come over as soon as possible. Honey Bunch's parents had offered to take them. They were dressing. "You're to tell the police if their prisoner is the man you saw in Barham," Stub's father said.

Aunt Carol told Honey Bunch to put on her play clothes while breakfast was being cooked. Then they could start off directly after eating.

By nine o'clock Honey Bunch, her father and mother, Norman, and Stub were on their way in the car. As they reached the Midville police station, Honey Bunch held her breath.

Would her lost puppy come bounding out to her?

CHAPTER XV

AN EXCHANGE OF PETS

Mr. Reilly was not in sight as Honey Bunch and Norman ran into the police station ahead of the others. They went directly to the captain's desk.

"I'm Honey Bunch Morton," the little girl said. "May I please have my puppy?"

The kindly captain looked down at her. "Now don't feel too bad, little miss. We found the man but not your dog."

Honey Bunch's lower lip began to tremble, and she had hard work to keep from crying. At this moment her parents and Stub came in, and Norman told them about Mr. Reilly.

"I'll have the prisoner, Stanley Jackner, brought in," the captain said.

In a few moments a policeman came from the back of the station with a man.

"He's the one!" Norman cried out. "He asked me if Honey Bunch would sell her pup."

Honey Bunch ran up to the prisoner. "Oh, what did you do with Mr. Reilly?" she asked. "Tell me where he is!"

"I don't know," Jackner answered.

Mr. Morton stepped forward. "But you admit taking my daughter's dog from the parade?"

The prisoner hung his head but finally said yes, he had. "I'd been looking for a trick dog to use in a carnival act," he said. "When I saw yours at the lumberyard and later on the float, I decided I had to have him. This boy here said your daughter wouldn't sell the dog, so I just took him. I didn't hurt him."

Jackner said that, as a matter of fact, he had taught the police puppy several new tricks.

"Where is he now?" Honey Bunch demanded. "I want him!"

"I don't know where he is," the man repeated.

"What do you mean?" Mr. Morton asked sternly.

"Just that," Jackner answered. "I sold him."

"Sold him!" Honey Bunch exclaimed.

"Yes. So that's why I don't know where he is."

Honey Bunch was so disappointed that she turned her head away. Norman and Stub felt very sorry for her. They wanted to help.

Norman faced the prisoner. "You'd better tell where Mr. Reilly is. I'm—I'm a good fighter, and if you don't—"

Mr. Morton laid his hand on Norman's shoulder. "I think this fellow will talk," he said. "Now tell us where you sold the dog."

Jackner said he had met some people along the road near Pennhurst. They were touring the country with a trailer. "There was a little girl with them who said she'd lost her police puppy. Her pop offered me a lot of money for your dog, so I sold him."

"Now I'll never get Mr. Reilly back!" Honey Bunch wailed.

Stub was not ready to give up. "Where were the trailer people going?" she asked Jackner.

"I don't know."

The prisoner now seemed genuinely sorry for Honey Bunch. Tears were rolling down her cheeks.

"I've got an idea," he said. "Maybe those folks will take in the carnival here. Why don't you go there and look?"

"Oh, yes, let's," Honey Bunch begged her parents.

After Mr. Morton had talked with the police captain a few minutes, he left the station with his wife and the children. They got in the car and drove at once to the carnival.

As they neared it, Honey Bunch said ex-

citedly, "Look! There's a trailer by the side
of the road. Maybe Mr. Reilly's in it!"

Daddy Morton stopped the car. The children hopped out and ran to the trailer. The
door was closed, and no one answered their
knock. And no dog's bark came from inside.

"I guess the people are at the carnival," said
Norman.

He and the girls climbed into the car again,
and in a few minutes Mr. Morton reached the
entrance. He parked the car.

How gay the carnival sounded! The visitors
could hear music from a merry-go-round and
children laughing. Mr. Morton bought tickets
and followed his group inside.

"Oh boy, this is swell!" said Norman, seeing
lots of booths with games to play. Then he remembered about the puppy. "Where shall we
look first, Mr. Morton?" he asked.

"I guess we'll just have to wander around,"
Honey Bunch's daddy replied.

"And hope we see Mr. Reilly," Honey Bunch
said.

They walked from place to place in the
grounds. There was not a dog at the carnival,
it seemed.

"Maybe they wouldn't allow Mr. Reilly in,"
Honey Bunch remarked to Norman and Stub.

But just then they heard a dog bark. Honey
Bunch said it was not her puppy's kind of bark.

"But now we know dogs can come in," she said hopefully.

They went on. No Mr. Reilly. Finally Mrs. Morton said the children should have some **fun** for a while, then hunt some more later.

"How about a ride on the merry-go-round?" she suggested.

"Oh, yes," said Norman, "and I want to treat." He ran to the booth and bought three tickets.

When the merry-go-round stopped the children hopped aboard. Norman decided to ride a lion and began to growl like one. Honey Bunch chose a swan and Stub a giraffe. As the platform started to move, the animals went up and down. The music from the caliope organ played loudly. Norman whipped his lion and growled even more fiercely.

When the ride was over, the children joined Mr. and Mrs. Morton. "Next I want to ride the Ferris wheel, please!" Stub said to the grownups. They stood watching the cars on the giant wheel go high into the air.

Norman glanced up at the top Ferris wheel car which was just turning past the highest point. "Boy, that's sure up in the sky," he said.

"The higher, the better!" Stub said gleefully. "Do you want to ride, Honey Bunch?"

"Oh, yes!"

"I do too," Norman said.

Mr. Morton bought tickets for all of them. When the Ferris wheel stopped to take on passengers, he and Norman got into one car. Honey Bunch and Stub rode with Mrs. Morton.

The Ferris wheel started. Up, up, up it went. When the two cars reached the top, **the** wheel suddenly stopped.

"This is to give us a better view!" said Stub, who had been on a Ferris wheel only a few days before.

How wonderful everything below them

looked! Flags waved. The red, blue, and yellow decorations on the booths made the carnival look very pretty.

"It's just like fairyland," said Honey Bunch.

But not for a minute had she forgotten her dog. The little girl's eyes roved over the scene below her, hoping to see him. She glanced down at the upturned faces of the people watching the Ferris wheel.

Suddenly she cried out, "Mother, look!" Honey Bunch pointed far below to a girl about eight years old standing beside the merry-go-round.

The girl held a police dog puppy under her arm! And it looked just like Mr. Reilly!

Mrs. Morton had a hard time holding her young daughter still. Honey Bunch wriggled around, crying, "I'm sure it's my puppy! Oh, Mother, we mustn't let that girl get away!"

By this time all the Mortons and Norman were convinced that the dog was Mr. Reilly. They must find out. It seemed as if the Ferris wheel would never start moving!

Norman stood up and yelled loudly, "Get us down!"

A few seconds later the Ferris wheel started its descent.

"Oh, hurry, hurry!" Honey Bunch cried, for they seemed to be going very slowly.

Finally her car reached the bottom. The attendant unlocked the door and the little girl dashed to the child who was holding the puppy.

The strange girl and the dog had their backs to Honey Bunch. But when she called, "Mr. Reilly!" the dog turned and leaped from the girl's arms.

Barking happily, he raced to his little mistress. Honey Bunch, almost beside herself with joy, knelt down to embrace her lost puppy.

"Oh, Mr. Reilly, I finally found you!" she said, hugging him tightly.

Mr. Reilly whimpered and jumped around on his hind legs. Then his pink tongue licked Honey Bunch's face.

By now the strange little girl had run up. "Who are you?" she asked.

Honey Bunch told her and said the puppy was hers.

"Yours?" the other girl repeated. "But he's mine. My name is Sue and my daddy bought him for me."

Norman and Stub and the grownups had crowded around. "You bet he's Honey Bunch's dog," Norman said and told how the pup had been stolen. "Come here, Mr. Reilly, and do your Hi-diddle-diddle trick."

The puppy trotted over to the small boy, wagging his tail in friendly fashion. "Now walk on your hind legs!" Norman commanded. Mr. Reilly did the trick well.

"I guess he is your dog," said Sue. Then a tear rolled down her cheek. "Now I've lost two police puppies."

Suddenly an idea came to Honey Bunch and Norman at the same instant. Together they said, "Did you have a police puppy who wore a red collar with a bell on it?"

"Yes, I did," Sue answered. "Do you know where he is?"

"He's in Pennhurst," said Norman.

"At Mr. and Mrs. Denton's," Honey Bunch added and told how she and Norman had gone there looking for Mr. Reilly.

"Oh, that's wonderful," said Sue. "Now I

won't mind giving up your puppy. Mine's a darling too. I'll go find Daddy and Mommy so they can take me to Pennhurst right away." She said good-by and hurried off.

"This is the most scrumptious day of my life," said Honey Bunch, as she hugged Mr. Reilly again.

"I think it calls for a celebration with ice cream," Daddy Morton said, grinning. "Let's go to that open-air restaurant over there. Then the pup can stay with us."

They walked to the place and found a table. Mr. Reilly sat on a chair between Honey Bunch and Norman. Everyone ordered vanilla ice cream, and the little girl said her pet would have that too. When it was served, the dog was given his in a real dog dish which the waitress set on the floor.

As they all ate, Stub looked at Honey Bunch. "You're extra happy, aren't you? You're smiling all the time."

"Yes, I am, Stub. And besides, a miss like me is as good as a smile."

"Aw, you're all mixed up, Honey Bunch," said Norman.

"I'm afraid she is," Daddy Morton agreed. "Honey Bunch means, 'A miss is as good as a mile.' But I like it better the way my little daughter says it."

Honey Bunch laughed. Then suddenly she

said, "Look at Mr. Reilly! He's so happy he's smiling too!"

The dog had glanced up. There was a curve of vanilla ice cream above his upper lip. He did look as if he were laughing.

Honey Bunch started to hum Hi-diddle-diddle. Norman, grinning, made up some new words. He sang loudly:

> *"Hi diddle diddle!*
> *Lady Clare and Norman's fiddle,*
> *Stub's cow jumped over the moon;*
> *Mr. Reilly laughed*
> *To see such sport*
> *And Mrs. Miller's dish*
> *Ran away with the spoon."*

The girls laughed, then Honey Bunch said, "That's good, Norman, and isn't it wonderful that my dog and cat will be together again?"

"With my fiddle," Norman added.

"And you can have my cow," Stub offered with a grin.

"But the moon," said Honey Bunch, "that belongs to everybody!"

You will meet Honey Bunch and Norman again, in an exciting seashore adventure. Be sure to share with them the fun and thrills that are awaiting HONEY BUNCH AND NORMAN ON LIGHTHOUSE ISLAND.